BLOOD LIKE GARNETS

LEIGH HARLEN

Blood Like Garnets by Leigh Harlen

Cover art & illustrations by Maria Nguyen

Cover design by Jared K. Fletcher

Interior layout and design by Jeff Powell

All inquiries should be addressed to:
TKO Studios, LLC.
1325 Franklin Avenue
Suite 545
Garden City, NY 11530.

TKO STUDIOS is a registered trademark.

Visit our website at www.tkopresents.com

First Edition
ISBN: 978-1-952203-30-5

Printed in the United States of America

CONTENTS

For Alison, who might be too scared to read this book, but without whom not a single word would have been written.

The New Flesh

The boy was going to be quite difficult to put back together. One mangled ear lay on the table next to his left cheek. A smear of angry, blistered flesh ran from his right hand to his left shoulder, where something had struck him, turning his flesh into grotesque streamers and providing an unwelcome view into the inner workings of his shoulder joint. The room was papered in expensive wallpaper, and heavy crimson curtains blocked sunlight and prying eyes, leaving only an antique lamp to see him by. A bouquet of little, yellow, marsh marigolds strove to bring cheer to the dim sickroom.

I sighed. I'd foolishly believed when his parents had said there was an accident, implying something more mundane, like perhaps a finger sliced off with a kitchen knife, or a bone broken by roughhousing with friends. The burn marks and mangled tissue told me he'd been playing with fireworks, and the faint odor of vodka wafting from his mouth paired with his shallow breaths told me he'd been drunk at the time. But, a wound was a wound, and I was a professional, so I sat beside him and slipped on a pair of clean gloves before removing my knitting needles and yarn from their sterile packaging.

Sometimes I missed the old days, when my needles were heavy and made of wood, with perfectly smooth spots worn where my fingers touched, instead of these lightweight, soulless, steel sticks. But, things change, knowledge accumulates, and a witch must keep up with the times, lest she end up a lonely, cackling madwoman, living deep in the woods and visited only by birds and impish children on a dare.

My yarn was softer than the softest silk and thinner than gossamer strands of a spider's web. But it knit into a fabric of unblemished flesh, strands of fibrous muscle, or solid, ivory chunks of bone. Safer than skin grafts and surgeries with none of the healing time. Well, almost none. They wouldn't replace the blood this boy had lost or erase any trauma or gnawing fear his injury planted in his brain. Time would have to do that work.

As I knit, the boy whimpered and sweat, but never once complained. "You're a good lad," I told him. "Your parents should be so proud of you."

I didn't say he was also an idiot who should leave explosives to the professionals, or at least the sober. No point in kicking him while he was down.

When I was done, his skin was whole, fresh, and pink as a baby's. He'd long since passed out, but his breathing had steadied and deepened. The young man would live to make stupid, reckless decisions another day. I dropped my gloves, needles, and the remains of thread into a small, sealable bag—I couldn't leave the yarn behind for regular people to use, or worse, *analyze*—and quietly let myself out.

As soon as his parents heard my footsteps creak on the luxurious, if scarred, mahogany floor, they flung themselves through the doorway and draped themselves over their patched-up son, crying and burbling words of relief and joy.

I waited impatiently until the clock down the hall chimed the hour and then cleared my throat.

The boy's mother stepped into the hall, her puffy, tearstained face now resolute and her hands on her hips. I steeled myself. It was going to be one of *those*.

"I hate to interrupt, but I'm sure we'd all rather I left as soon as possible," I said, hoping that maybe if I appeared reasonable and not like the villain she'd created in her head, she wouldn't put up a fight.

She reached into her deceptively deep pocket and pulled out a checkbook.

"That is not the price we agreed on."

"You cannot possibly expect me to pay what we agreed to. It's monstrous. We were desperate, and you took advantage."

"Perhaps I did." I most certainly did, but her desperation, her need, was no greater than mine. "But your son was also in much worse shape than you led me to believe, and despite that, I'm not raising my prices. Be glad I didn't take the opportunity to renegotiate." I lowered my voice and clipped my words until they were razor sharp with warning.

She handed me a pen and her checkbook. "Just write whatever number you will accept. We'll pay it. Surely you can buy what you need from someone else with enough money."

I threw her pen and checkbook against the wall, and some mean little part of me took great satisfaction in seeing her jump and step back from me. "You'd ask a stranger to pay my *monstrous* price?"

She cast her eyes down, perhaps ashamed, but then hardened again. "Yes. Find someone who doesn't have a son she wants to see get married. Someone who's not…"

"Someone who's not what? As important as you are? For every minute longer you argue with me, I will double my price. And if you still refuse, you should know, my work gives me a permanent connection to your son. What is given can be easily taken away." I waved my hand in the air, and she paled, believing that I was casting a spell. It was nonsense. I could no more magically rip the knitted flesh and muscle from her son than I could from her. But it was effective nonsense.

"We could call the police." But her shoulders hunched, and her voice was hollow. We both knew she'd lost.

"You could. And then you could explain to them how your underage son got ahold of alcohol and illegal fireworks and blew himself up. And then you opted for the more certain and aesthetically pleasing work of illegal witchcraft over a proper hospital. Will you be the one paying me, or perhaps the boy's father?" Better to push instead of giving her time to recover.

"Mom?" the boy called.

She glanced over her shoulder, desperate to return to him. She looked back at me. "I will. He doesn't know." Her voice was small and defeated, and it made me feel more like a villain than her haughty blustering did.

I beckoned her around the corner. There was no reason her son needed to know the price of his recklessness. She followed.

"Will it hurt?"

"Yes," I said.

She straightened her spine and raised her chin and nodded.

I removed a small glass vial from my beat-up leather bag and then reached out toward her face. She flinched, but then settled as my hand cupped the left side of her head, just behind the ear. Eyes closed, I began to pull. Warm, tickling energy flowed into my hand. She gasped, and a soft whimper escaped her lips before she bit down. Her entire body was a knot of rigid, pained tension, but she was silent. I respected her for that, she was tough even if she was a pampered, conniving, weasel of a woman.

When I released her, she sagged, sweating against the wall. New streaks of white graced her temples, and the lines around her eyes and mouth deepened. I held ten years of her life in my hand, a roiling, iridescent ball like an oil slick, and pushed it gently into the vial and closed it with a stopper.

"Now get out," she said, voice raspy.

I didn't argue. I left the way I came in, through the back door so none of the neighbors could see me.

A clucking huddle of chickens greeted my homecoming.

"A good evening to you too, ladies." Most of them were ancient when it came to chickens and hardly laid eggs anymore, but they did keep the yard clear of ticks, so they more than earned their food and maintenance.

They followed me until I grabbed the stale bread from the basket next to the door and tossed it into the overgrown grass for them.

I turned at the sound of a honk. A rusting car drove by, and my nearest neighbor, Sammie, stuck her arm through the open window to wave. She and her son lived about a thirty minute walk down a gravel path through the woods and were the closest neighbors I had.

Sammie wasn't a witch like me, but she was an odd woman who kept a herd of goats. A lot of people gossiped that she'd killed her husband, though she'd confessed to me after a shared bottle of wine that he'd taken up with her sister and she'd kicked them both out of her house. I liked her and waved back, the moment of friendliness taking the bitter edge off my day.

I finished feeding the chickens and went inside. Home was small. Just one bedroom, that I now kept closed and locked so no guests or burglars could stumble upon my project. There was also a kitchen with about three whole feet of counter space, a bathroom with a shower so narrow I barely fit inside, and the living room, which also functioned as a library, study, dining room, and sleeping quarters. Once upon a time I would have called it cozy and warm, but now it was cluttered with dusty books, the corners draped in cobwebs. About half of the lights had gone out, and I'd not bothered to replace the bulbs. Herbs grew in clay pots on every available counter or tabletop.

I opened the refrigerator and carefully placed the unopened spools of yarn into the vegetable crisper. Each shelf was full of the materials I blended together to spin my yarn. The bottom shelf was stacked heavy with bones like kindling for a fire. The second shelf was filled with fatty livers, meaty hearts, squishy brains, loops of intestine, and all the other internal bits that made a body live. The third shelf was for strings and slabs of muscle, tendon, and ligaments. And the top shelf buckled under the weight of sheets upon sheets of flesh. I kept the odds and ends, eyeballs, veins, and arteries in the butter drawer. So far, no one had figured out how to knit nerves into being from nothingness. That work mostly relied on coaxing growth from what already existed.

I grabbed several skeins of yarn and my bag and went to the back bedroom. The key hung permanently around my neck, and I had to crouch low so that the key could reach despite the short chain. It clicked, and I turned the knob and stepped inside, locking it behind me.

"Hello, sweetheart," I whispered, tender and reverent.

My project—my son, though I tried to think of him in objectifying terms lest seeing his shattered bones and pulp of organs drive me mad—lay under a thin, golden yellow sheet peppered with lurid, smiling cartoon bees. For a long moment, I leaned against the door and tried to pretend he was sleeping.

I'd never been good at lying to myself. With a sigh, I pulled my chair away from the spinning wheel, dragged it to the bed and sat down next to my boy. For him, I used my old needles. Sturdy and carved from silvery-white birch, the tree with the most connection to life, death, and resurrection. It was less sanitary, but for this, I needed more of the old magic.

I pulled the sheet away, and a small, involuntary moan escaped my lips. My son. My boy. His sweet, beautiful smile turned into a lifeless, rigid, mockery of a peaceful sleep. His quick and clever hands, stilled and broken. It took me two months to find what remained of him. Most of him, the parts that weren't already shattered, had been eaten by animals.

The old rage bubbled inside me. I tried so hard to be detached. I needed to be in order to work. So that I could do the things I needed to do to put him back together again. But God, that rage was still so hot; if someone cut me, my blood should hiss and sizzle and steam.

(What kind of man, what kind of father could...?)(No. That line of thought led nowhere good. Nowhere productive.)

Moonlight dripped like liquid silver through the fluttering curtain, illuminating the red of the exposed muscles of his stomach. Blood swooshed through tubes all around him, oxygenating his blood and pumping it back inside. He was almost finished and whole and yet not alive. Not yet. He should be. If this was working, he should be alive. He had all the necessary pieces for respiration and a beating heart, but he remained still and silent. Worse, my work was slowed as bits of tissue necrosis broke through the magic and science of my work, and I had to make repairs.

I breathed deeply of the air that smelled like preserving chemicals and flesh on the edge of rot and began to work. Almost transparent thread knitting up into soft peach skin.

When my hands began aching, and my eyes felt like sandpaper with sleep, I set aside my needles and took the vial of life I'd earned today. I uncorked the lid and poured it into my hands, where it settled like an unwholesome, sickly, liquid rainbow. I rubbed it gently between my palms and massaged it into my son's cold skin, focusing the most on the new flesh and the bits that were beginning to blacken and necrotize.

As I began to doze in my chair, his left hand twitched. My heart shot up into my throat, and I watched, breath held, hardly daring to hope. But, his chest didn't rise, and his eyes didn't flutter. Sometimes muscles spasmed as they passed into and out of death's rigor. I touched his hand gently and silently wished for him to come back to me before pulling my feet onto the chair and curling up to sleep, even though I knew my back would scream at me for it tomorrow.

Whatever woke me was a mystery, but my eyes snapped open, and I sat bolt upright in my chair. Everything was silent except for a lone, frantic clucking from outside. I jumped to my feet and grabbed my shotgun from the locked cabinet. Witchcraft was a useful defense, but if some animal got at my chickens, I'd take the reliability of my shotgun.

At first, everything appeared to be in order. The yard was empty and quiet, the moon shone down, full and bright, illuminating a mess of white feathers almost hidden behind the coop. I crept forward, shotgun pressed firmly to my shoulder.

My worst fears were confirmed when I saw smears and splatters of blood staining the tan wall. White feathers. That had to be poor Tricks. My heart sunk, maybe it was silly, but I'd loved that fucking hen. She hadn't laid an egg in more than a year, and she was as mean as a rattlesnake having a real bad day, but she'd been with me when I finally kicked my husband out, and she'd been with me when my son—

I shook off the memories and went to check on the other chickens. I hoped they were safe, if terrified, huddled together in the coop. The coop door looked fine, but when I got closer, I saw it had been ripped off the hinges and now leaned against the frame as if someone wanted to hide the damage.

My grip tightened on the shotgun. Foxes didn't traditionally try to cover up their crimes. I pulled the door away and let it drop to the ground with a muffled thud. The remaining chickens greeted me with shrill, panicked clucks. It was dark, but the brilliant moon was enough to make it clear that Tricks hadn't been the only victim. The inside of the coop was a chicken abattoir. Only two birds remained, huddled together, half-buried in hay and bloodied feathers. My two little brown hens, Mish and Mash. Sisters I'd rescued from a neighbor who'd gotten in over their head with chickens they had no idea how to care for.

All I could think was that I couldn't leave them out here in the remains of their murdered flock, and I couldn't stay out here, cleaning blood off the walls and pitching hay in the middle of the night. I unloaded my gun so I didn't accidentally shoot myself in the ass, slung it over one shoulder, and scooped both panicked chickens up into one arm and brought them into the house for the night.

Just as I opened the door, something moved out of the corner of my eye. I whirled as a small, pale shape running on all fours disappeared behind the house. Whatever it was, it was too fast, too hunched and small to be a person. A coyote, perhaps, though I hadn't heard of them in this area. My chest loosened a little with relief. It was horrible, and I was going to mourn my chickens tomorrow. But a coyote was nothing that threatened me.

I locked my two chickens up in the bathroom, where the chicken shit would be confined and easiest to clean up, with a bit of toast, a bowl of food, and water.

After I'd locked the gun back up, I stretched out on the living room couch and tried to go back to sleep.

I spent the next few days cleaning the yard and coop of blood and feathers, fixing the coop, and adding a heavy lock. Mish and Mash would return to being free-range during the day when they regained their confidence, but in the meantime, and at night, nothing that couldn't operate wire cutters was getting in.

At night I knitted flesh into my dead son's abdomen and slept fitfully. I couldn't shake the feeling that something was moving around outside at night. It was pure paranoia and hy-pervigilance. But whenever a shadow fell across the window, a twig snapped, or the floorboards creaked as the house settled, I snapped awake.

I lay on the living room couch, my eyes closed and count-ing backwards from 1,000 in an effort to sleep when a scraping sound brought me to full alert. I didn't move, just lay rigid on the couch, listening intently.

A shadowed figure moved in front of my window. It moved slowly, stopping for long stretches before taking a cautious step closer, the dark shadow filling more of the window with each stalking step. I held my breath and slipped off the couch, keep-ing low even though losing sight of the shape in my window made me want to scream. When I stood just beneath the ledge, I crouched and slowly moved the curtain out of the way.

The instant the curtains moved, the thing ran. I yanked the curtain all the way open in time to see a figure, small, hunched, and pale, flee into the trees. Fingerprints and larger grease marks, like someone had pressed their face against the glass repeated-ly, covered the lower third of the window. I rubbed my arms to soothe my creeping skin. Something or someone had been watching me sleep.

I could alert the police, ask them to do a search of the woods. But they'd been worse than useless when I tried to get help in keeping my husband away from Johnny and me. If not for their 'help,' Johnny wouldn't have been at his father's house at all. No, I couldn't have cops tramping around my yard, making insinuations about the type of woman I must be to have a dead son, to do witchcraft, to live alone, to so publicly proclaim myself as 'other.' I'd have to deal with whatever this was myself.

But first, breakfast. I wasn't going to get anything done on an empty stomach and uncaffeinated. I set coffee to brew and began frying eggs and toasting bread with butter. I gazed brood-ily out the window, trying to decide what type of person would kill my chickens and creep around my house at night. Some kind of murderous madman who just saw an opportunity? Someone with a grudge against me personally? Perhaps an angry client or just a witch-hating fanatic.

"Mommy?"

I was so lost in thought and encased in my own loneliness that the familiar voice and the heartrending word didn't register until he spoke again.

"Mommy, I'm hungry."

Suddenly the world was too slow, like I was trapped in molasses, as I turned towards the bedroom door.

Johnny stood there, bleary-eyed and alive. His bare tummy pink and new, except for a slice like a piece of pie that showed the layers of skin and the nauseating movement of muscles and ligaments. He rubbed the edges of the hole absently, as if it itched, and I had a brief, terrifying thought that he would scratch himself wide open.

"Baby," I breathed the word like a prayer before I ran to him, dropped to my knees, and wrapped my arms around his warm little body.

He squirmed in my arms, and I reluctantly released him. His big eyes were darker and sadder than I remembered. But he was alive. My boy was alive. I hugged him once more, quick and tight, and released him before he could protest.

"I'm hungry," he reiterated, his eyes big and plaintive.

"Of course, baby. Let me get you something to eat."

I scrambled the eggs I'd been frying for myself and added cheese and butter, just the way he liked. How much did he remember about what happened? I couldn't even imagine how to help him process being murdered by his own father. If he didn't remember, did he really need to know?

"Here you go." I set the eggs in front of him while I sat across from him, with buttered toast and coffee. I was too stunned to eat or drink, or really to do anything other than stare at him while he poked at his breakfast with his fork as if it were the first time he'd ever seen eggs.

"Johnny, sweetheart, how do you feel?" I asked, after we'd sat in silence for what felt like an eternity.

"Hungry." His voice was heavy with need and longing and resignation.

"Then eat your eggs, they're one of your favorites," I said, trying so hard to sound cheerful and normal, hiding the thousands of complicated feelings running through me. These feelings made me want to either sit in uncomprehending silence and stare at him, or wrap him in a hug, dance around squealing, and never let him go ever again.

He shook his head. "They don't taste good."

"Hm." I stood and took a bite of his eggs. "Tastes fine to me."

He gazed at me balefully.

"What would you like to eat, then? I have some frozen waffles."

He wrinkled his nose in disgust. It was cute, and I was too relieved to be annoyed at his newfound pickiness.

"We could go out for breakfast." I wanted to take the suggestion back as soon as I said it. If we went into town, I was going to have to explain how my dead son was with me. Hypervisibility was one of the perils of being an object of sensationalism in a medium-sized town.

"Too loud," he said.

I tried not to look too relieved. "What would you like, then?"

He shook his head in that familiar way he did when he wanted to say something and was deeply frustrated because the feeling was just too big for his six-year-old vocabulary to convey.

"That's okay. When you decide on something, let me know. Is that okay?"

He nodded, and a trace of my sweet boy's smile flitted across his face. It made me want to break down crying at his feet.

"What would you like to do? You want to play a game? Color?"

"Can we play hide and seek?"

The last thing I wanted to do was play a game where the point was to lose sight of him for even a second, but how could I tell him no?

"Sure, baby. Do you want to hide first?"

"Count to a hundred," he demanded.

"How about fifty?" I countered.

He nodded, sage and serious, then gestured at me to cover my eyes.

I obliged. "One… two… three…"

We spent several days doing little but playing hide and seek. Somehow Johnny had gotten braver, hiding outside in the woods that used to terrify him, instead of under his bed or amidst a pile of laundry in his closet. And he developed a strange habit of sneaking out of bed at night to eat. He never admitted to doing it and wouldn't eat anything that I tried to feed him during the day, but I heard him rummaging through the kitchen while I slept on the couch. He wasn't starving. If anything, he was getting healthier. Rosy-cheeked and plump thighed. We'd have to talk about it eventually, but for now, I was just glad he was alive.

A knock on the door startled me from my breakfast reverie. I stood and looked through the window to see Sammie and her son, Frederick. Never Fred. Never Freddy. Frederick.

I hesitated. I wasn't sure if I was ready to explain Johnny. Or maybe I just wasn't ready to let the world into our little bubble just yet.

He looked up at me from his coloring book. "Who is it, Mommy?"

I gave him a reassuring smile. "Sammie and Frederick. Do you want to say hi?"

He slid off his chair and nodded.

I took a deep breath and opened the door, steeling myself for a lengthy explanation.

"Oh, thank God, Rose. Can you watch Frederick for me this afternoon? I've got an emergency. Something got at the goats last night and managed to kill one. She had a kid who's now doing poorly, and I've got to spend the day with the vet and doing feedings. I'd feel better if Frederick had someone to keep a better eye on him than I can right now."

Her words came out in a torrent. All I could do was nod as the boy was pushed gently towards me. She gave him a quick peck on the forehead, "Be good for Rose." Then she turned heel and started jogging away.

"Okay, well. Come on in, Frederick." I turned and was startled to see Johnny standing immediately behind me, head cocked to the side. He and Frederick had been the same age, but despite Sammie and my best efforts, the boys never took to one another. Johnny was sensitive and quiet and liked coloring and cataloging birds. Frederick was also quiet, but more inclined to building model cars and playing video games.

So I was surprised to see the look of unabashed interest on Johnny's face. Frederick's mouth dropped. "My mama said you died," he blurted out.

I cringed and watched Johnny's face. There was no shock or stunned horror, this wasn't news to him. "Yes. My daddy is bad. Mommy fixed me."

Frederick seemed to contemplate this before nodding. He was, after all, only six. And in his extremely limited life experience, 'Daddy was bad, and Mommy fixed things' made perfect sense.

"Do you want to play hide and seek?" Johnny asked.

Frederick bit his lower lip. Hide and seek was not his sort of game, but he was polite. I considered trying to rescue him, but at last, he said, "Okay. If we can play Lego next."

I smiled at seeing Johnny nod. Maybe it would be a good thing that Frederick was here for the afternoon.

Babysitting Frederick for the afternoon turned into a sleepover. I tucked the boys into bed, where they seemed happy as two clams in one another's company. I slept on the couch, feeling content that not only was my son back, but things were returning, if not to normal, to a new kind of normal. He still did all of his eating alone, and on the sly. I wondered if it had been a meal gone bad that had been the spark on the tinder of his father's abusive rage that led to his murder. But he was happy and playing games and even making a new friend. Everything was going to be fine.

I woke in the very early hours of morning while the moon and stars still hung in the sky with a powerful need to pee. Bleary-eyed, I fumbled to the bathroom. On my way back to bed, I quietly opened the door to reassure myself that Johnny was there and that he was breathing.

The bed was empty except for mussed blankets, and the window was wide open, the screen missing completely.

"Johnny," I shouted, "Johnny, where are you?" I ran to the bed and pulled the blankets off, as if he might be hiding under them. He wasn't there. He wasn't in the bedroom at all.

Neither was Frederick. I tried to calm the frantic disarray of my thoughts by assuring myself that the boys had probably snuck out, part of some silly child's game.

I slipped on shoes and ran outside, still in my pajamas. The air was cool, and the breeze flapped the loose fabric, but it wasn't quite truly cold.

"Johnny? Frederick?" I shouted as I stumbled over the uneven ground.

A pale shape, impossibly fast and silent, disappeared, dragging something behind it into the woods. I chased after it. Branches slashed my face and arms and ripped at my hair, but still, I ran. A root tripped me up, and I stumbled, losing my footing, and tumbled over the lip of the earth and into a small valley. Just a chuckling creek surrounded by rocky earth and sparse scrub. I was about to climb back out and continue searching when pebbles clattered and plunked into the water.

I followed the sound to an eroded divot in the steep slope of earth beside the creek. I held my breath and stepped forward to block whatever was in there from escaping.

Moonlight illuminated a pale, naked shape, face hidden and crouched over a small body dressed in fire truck pajamas.

The thing jerked its head, ripping loose a chunk of flesh from poor little Frederick's abdomen. It threw its head back, and swallowed the flesh whole, like a bird of prey. Frederick's narrow chest rose and fell in shallow breaths, and he waved weakly, as if still trying to fight the thing off.

Blood smeared a mouth more familiar than my own, his sweet, sad, dark eyes now closed in apparent ecstasy.

"Johnny?" I whispered.

He froze and opened his eyes. "Hi, Mommy."

"Baby, what are you doing?" The question was inane. It was obvious what I was seeing, but it was so impossible, so alien, that it bounced right off me.

"I'm sorry I went outside at night. I'm hungry, Mommy. I'm so hungry." He jumped over Frederick, quick and easy like a cat, and buried his blood and gore covered face in my side. "Don't be mad, Mommy. I didn't mean to make a mess."

Reflexively I patted his back and whispered, "It's okay, baby. Mommy's not mad." All the time and energy and magic I'd put into bringing him back had gone horribly wrong.

Bones littered the ground around Frederick's body. Most picked clean and gnawed. A few looked human. There was one bloody stump of goat leg torn from a body that was who knew where.

"It's okay. It's okay. Mommy will figure out what to do," I murmured.

Frederick choked and gurgled on his own blood. The boy might still be saved if he could live long enough to get to the house. I knelt and gathered him gently into my arms.

"Let's go home, baby."

On our walk back to the house, my arms aching with the surprising weight of Frederick's small body and his little fingers grabbing reflexively and tenaciously at me, I debated what to do. No one I knew had managed to do what I'd done in bringing Johnny back to life. There were no books on the topic that weren't ancient and riddled with nonsense and falsities. I was on my own here.

But as I watched Johnny, naked as a jaybird and slick with blood, skip brightly through the moon-soaked woods, I knew nothing would take him from me. I would do anything for him. And that, in itself, was a kind of decision.

Sammie screamed and cried and threatened when I told her that Frederick had taken off in the night. He probably got homesick and tried to find his own way home. But she left, out into the woods, to search.

She wouldn't find him. Not ever, hopefully. After bringing Johnny home and bathing him, I'd gone back to his lair to clean away any sign that Johnny or Frederick had ever been there. I scattered the bones and the gnawed goat leg throughout the woods, where they could be blamed on coyotes. I weighed down any pieces that might be human and let them sink into the deepest part of the river that cut through the forest. With luck, the current would drag them along the bottom, unseen, all the way to the ocean. Perhaps I should have done for Sammie what I did for myself and for so many other mothers.

No. It was better this way. I repeated that to myself over and over again. I'd make sure Johnny was fed and that he didn't need to eat anyone else's child. It was a mercy what I was doing. Johnny was alive, and that was the only thing that mattered. I loved him, and I would do anything for him.

When Sammie's shouts became almost inaudible, I beckoned Johnny out of the shadows, took his tiny hand in mine and led him into the bedroom, where his lifeless body had haunted me for so long.

Frederick sat up in bed, his abdomen pink with freshly knit skin, and his eyes bulging as he cried soundlessly and tugged at the ropes that held him to the bed. Johnny had torn his vocal cords, and out of mercy to us both, I'd left them that way.

"Now, Johnny, you can't ever let him stop breathing, okay? Mommy can only bring him back for you if he doesn't die. We don't want to have to hurt anyone else. Do you understand?"

He nodded, his eyes casting back and forth between Frederick and me. "I'm hungry, Mommy."

"Okay, baby. Just remember what I said." I left the room and closed the door against the sounds of scuffling, grunts of delight, and wet slurping bites.

Lazarus Taxon

Entry 1

[Wind. Soft murmurs and instrumental music. The low rumble of a heavy vehicle on gravel.]

Karin: What follows are the audio notes and interviews conducted by freelance science journalist, Karin Reese, that's me, duh, starting May 22nd at 0900. I will be meeting with Dr. Renee Harris, as soon as I figure out how the hell to get there, to talk about her discovery of a colony of little brown bats previously believed to be extinct.

Future Karin, here's a quick audio draft for the opening of the article:

In a sealed cavern of the Crystal Cave, once popular with tourists and school groups, scientists have discovered a colony of *Myotis lucifugus*, or more commonly, the little brown bat. The discovery is credited to Dr. Renee Harris, a researcher at the University of Wisconsin. Dr. Harris has been studying the Crystal Cave ecosystem for nearly forty years and has watched firsthand as its once healthy and numerous bat colonies died out. The little brown bat was believed to be extinct, with only a single animal living in captivity, named Lonely Eric by the staff at the Detroit Zoo.

Little brown bats had long been threatened due to white-nose syndrome, a fungal infection that hit many bat species hard. It looked as though populations might recover when the world was hit with the mass die-out of the insects that comprised their diet.

How these bats have survived in this cavern with no apparent source of food has scientists baffled, and has created a stir of hope that maybe the insect die-off wasn't the complete extinction event previously feared.

[Car door slamming, soft footsteps on earthy ground.]

[Click.]

Karin: Dr. Harris, do you have a theory? Some have suggested a colony of insects might be trapped inside as well. If so, would it be possible to reintroduce them to ecosystems outside the cave?

Dr. Harris: You're in my way. [Scraping and popping from the microphone.]

Karin: Asshole. Sorry, just edit that out later.

[Click.]

Entry 2

Karin: Still May 22nd, at about 1305.

Dr. Harris and her team are using a robot with a camera to explore the cavern. The grad students have been calling the robot Alfred after the Batman character, though it looks more like a snake than a person. It's cute, or deeply unsettling, depending on your opinion of snakes, but perfectly designed to fit through small spaces and navigate uncertain terrain. Graduate student Amanda Liu is approaching the sealed entrance to create an opening for the robot.

And there it goes! Alfred is inside, and now we await what data it sends back.

[Cheers are interrupted by indistinct, angry shouting.]

Dr. Harris: You can't be here. Someone, escort this man away.

Karin: What's going on?

Unknown man: Get the fuck out of here! [inaudible] bricked up for a reason. Rabies and diseases—

Grad Student: Sir. I can assure you, the chances of you or your cattle getting rabies or any other diseases from bats are very slim so long as you leave them in peace.

Dr. Harris: If your cows are getting sick, go home and yell at your feed supplier, that's a much more likely cause. I have work to do.

[Indistinct yelling grows fainter.]

Karin: Well, that was—

Dr. Harris: That was sensationalist horseshit is what it was.

Karin: It sounds like it's not the first time you've heard it.

Dr. Harris: It's not. Everything on this planet is dying. People want something to blame, and if they can't blame anything else for the die-offs, at least they can blame bats for giving their cows rabies or whatever nonsense they picked up on some corner of the internet. Bats have always been an easy target, hell, these ones might only be alive because someone tried to kill them all by sealing the cave entrance. I've walked into more than one cave full of nothing but skeletons because some ignorant asshole bricked up the entrance or doused the place in poison.

Karin: That's awful.

Dr. Harris: It is. Frankly, human action killed this planet and wiped out damn near every bat species in the world. And most people don't even make the connections between their absence and the loss of the plants they used to pollinate, and the species that relied on them for food, and all the other deaths that rippled out through the food web from there. Now get that out of my face so I can pay attention.

Karin: Thanks for your time, Doctor. [Soft and directly into the microphone.] Wow. Most words I've gotten out of her all day. If I didn't think she'd throw something at me, I'd make the point that good science communication can be key in quelling illogical fears like this before they get that heated. But hey, what do I know?

[Ambient sound and chatter.]

Dr. Harris: We've got visual!

[Cheers.]

Karin: We can see the bats. Wow, there's so many of them. I can't even count how many. They're all hanging from the ceiling, they're moving, wings fluttering on every surface. As far as I can tell, they seem healthy. There are small bones on the floor, I can't tell what they belong to, but I'm sure we'll know soon. Is it possible they adapted their food source from insects to small animals? There used to be a species of bat that adapted to eating scorpions instead of moths, so mice wouldn't be such a leap I'd think. If that's what happened, where did those animals come from?

[Click.]

Entry 3

Karin: [Whispering.] It is May 23rd at 0700, and we are looking at video records taken by Alfred.

Dr. Harris: It's extremely unlikely, but given what I'm looking at, it is indeed possible.

Unknown voice: They just don't live that long. Must be mistaken. Fur discoloration or bad video footage. I've been telling you for years to use bands.

Dr. Harris: Those are my brands. I know my own work, Isaac.

Karin: Can you explain what it means to find a branded bat?

Dr. Harris: In this case, freeze-branding. Putting bands on bats, like we do birds, is dangerous to them. No, don't argue with me, Isaac. It is, and you know it. Anyway, that's why my preference is freeze-branding. They do it with cattle, too. It's well tested. Ignore, Isaac. He's just an ornery old ass. Instead of heat like you might be used to seeing in movies and such, we use liquid nitrogen. It makes the fur grow back without pigment. And Alfred got a close-up of this bat, and I branded her thirty-six years ago.

Karin: What is the lifespan of the little brown bat?

Dr. Harris: Usually? Let's say five to ten years. The oldest known in the wild was thirty-four.

Karin: So thirty-six is extremely old.

Dr. Harris: Yes.

Karin: Impossibly old?

Dr. Harris: Apparently not.

Karin: And were you able to figure out what they've been eating?

[Twenty seconds of ambient sound and fingers drumming.]

Dr. Harris: As near as I can tell, one another.

Karin: Wait, are you saying they're cannibal bats?

Dr. Harris: [Voice turns harsh.] I swear to God if you title your article that you will never go on an expedition with me again.

[Click.]

Entry 4

[Indistinct screaming and high-pitched screeches. Thumps of something fleshy on canvas.]

Karin: [Whispering.] I don't know what's happening. I was asleep, and then I heard shouting, and something hit my tent. I thought someone was throwing clumps of dirt. Oh. Oh my god. The bats. They're streaming out of the hole we made to get the camera inside. It's amazing. I can see one. It's so small I can't make out its features from here. The camera hole was smaller. I don't know how it fits. Oh shit.

[*Hungry*]

Karin: Oh. Oh shit. Someone is bleeding. One of the grad students, I think. It looks like they were hit in the head. [Relieved sigh.] Looks like they're okay, though. Wow. I wish I had a video camera. You should see this. It's like a cyclone of bats pouring out of the cavern and into the sky. It's beautiful.

[*Blood*]

Karin: I can't help but feel happy for them. They've been in that cave for so long. Long enough to start eating one another to survive. Most of them their entire lives. I hope they can survive outside of it now.

[*SoHungryBloodHungryHungryHungry*]

[Click.]

Entry 5

Karin: It's May 24th, about 0315. [Yawns.] I'm here in the tent that Dr. Harris has turned into a temporary specimen closet and lab. She is about to perform a necropsy on one of the bats who died on their way out of the cave last night.

Dr. Harris: [Voice slightly muffled.] I have a suspicion we might be looking at rabies. You see the amount of saliva production?

Karin: The student who was bitten last night, they were vaccinated, right? And would that mean the entire colony is infected?

Dr. Harris: Yes, they were, and not necessarily. Starting the incision. [Eight minutes of silence.] Huh.

Karin: What is it?

Dr. Harris: The heart is extremely enlarged. [Scraping and heavy breathing.] Stomach contents include blood and fur. Mostly blood. [Several minutes of ambient sound.] The brain is visibly inflamed. [Metallic clinking and indistinct muttering.] A sample stained with hematoxylin and eosin shows evidence of encephalomyelitis.

Karin: What does that mean?

Dr. Harris: It means we need to send the other sample to a lab and quickly. [Latex gloves snap.]

Karin: Because it's rabies?

Dr. Harris: Because it's not. It shares some similarities, but as far as I can tell, that animal should have been dead long before it ever flew out of that cave.

[Click.]

Entry 6

Karin: It's May 24th at 1430. Dr. Harris sent samples for testing to Madison and is on the phone with colleagues there now. While we wait, I have with me graduate student Terry Rodowski. Terry was the student who was bitten last night. How are you feeling, Terry?

Terry: [High-pitched laughter.] Not great, Karin.

Karin: Can you elaborate?

Terry: Not really. [Giggling that turns into labored breathing.] Besides, why do you want to know? You always have that recorder with you. Are you recording right now? Who are you giving those tapes to?

Karin: What? I don't understand. I'm writing an article about the discovery. You know that.

Terry: Fuck, is it hot in here?

Karin: Do you want a drink of water? I have a bottle. Here.

Terry: Get that away from me. [A clink followed by the sound of metal striking rock.]

Unknown voice: You really shouldn't be in here, Miss.

Terry: [Mimicking.] You really shouldn't be in here, Miss. Sorry. I'm just very hungry. [Giggling.]

[Click.]

Entry 7

Karin: Still May 24th. Now 1900. I'm here with Dr. Harris. [Voice trembling.] Well, Doctor, you got results back from Madison.

Dr. Harris: Yes.

Karin: What are we dealing with?

Dr. Harris: I don't know.

Karin: It's not rabies.

Dr. Harris: No. Though it does appear to operate similarly. It's a virus that affects the nervous system. Given the drooling and high concentration of virus in the saliva, it seems likely that is how it is spread. And it causes encephalitis, that is, uh, swelling of the brain.

Karin: How is it different?

Dr. Harris: Well, for one, it causes a degree of encephalitis that should be fatal but is not. Other than that, I don't know how different the effects might be. All I can say is that though it has some similarities, it is a completely different virus.

Karin: Are we in any danger?

Dr. Harris: I don't think so. I can't speculate about Mr. Rodowski's condition or prognosis. [Twelve seconds of silence. Dr. Harris clears her throat.] But, if it operates as we think, we are probably safe. If the other bats return to the cavern, we will seal it back up. They survived many long years in there, and will probably survive a bit longer while we figure out what to do. If they don't return—

Karin: Doctor?

Dr. Harris: [Sighs.] If they don't return, they'll have to be eradicated.

Karin: And Terry? Is he dangerous? Could he infect others?

Dr. Harris: His behavior has been erratic. But that is to be expected with encephalitis. The swelling can cause a wide range of personality changes from rage to paranoia, and so far, he is exhibiting all the above and then some. But, if my theory is right and it is spread through saliva like rabies, well, except for organ transplants, humans don't spread rabies to other humans. Human teeth are not built for tearing flesh the way say, a dog's teeth are.

Karin: [Nervous laughter.] So, don't let him bite me or give me a kidney?

Dr. Harris: Basically. And he stays quarantined in his tent from now on. Seriously, I know you went to talk to him. No more of that. Look. Just. Turn that off for a minute, would you?

[Click.]

Entry 8

Karin: May 24th at 2100. I'm trying to get to sleep, but I can't stop thinking about what Dr. Harris said. I can't quote her on this in an article, or she'll deny it. But she thinks it's possible that whatever this virus is, it's what allowed the bats to stay alive. Or not stay alive exactly, but maybe it's animating them. Like that fungus in tropical forests that takes over ants.

There's something else, though. I was reviewing my notes from the past couple of days, and in the recording when the bats first emerged from the cave there was a voice. A voice that wasn't mine. But that's crazy, right? I didn't hear it last night when it was happening, but everything was chaos. I was distracted. But okay, say someone was talking, and I just didn't notice at the time. Who was it? It didn't sound like anyone I know, but they must have been right beside me. It—didn't even sound human. But that's ridiculous.

Tell you what, future Karin. We fucked up good going into journalism. Should have listened to dad and gone to law school.

[Click.]

Entry 9

[Twenty-one seconds of screaming. Panting.]

[*Hungry*]

[*Blood*]

[*BloodBloodBlood*]

[*FoodHungryBlood*]

[Sixty-four seconds of screaming, panting, and ambient noise.]

[Click.]

Entry 10

Karin: [Fifteen seconds of crying.] I don't know how to explain what happened last night. Terry escaped quarantine, and the bats returned. But this time, it wasn't just one fly-by nip on their way out into the dark.

Okay, pull yourself together, Karin. I need to describe exactly what happened. [Clears throat.] I was in my tent, trying to sleep when I heard shouting. I went outside and saw Terry. He was naked, running. He was screaming something about it being too hot. No. To be exact, he said his blood was scalding. Then the bats came. At first, I thought they were trying to get back into the cave. But they swarmed the camp. I don't know how many. Hundreds of thousands, I think, but honestly, what good is a visual estimate of any number over a few hundred, right? Well, in my scientific opinion, it was a shit ton more than a few hundred.

Dr. Harris came out of her tent, and Terry jumped on her. He was a small guy, and she is— was a big woman, but he knocked her flat on her back. He was shrieking and snapping at her neck like a wolf. She had a scalpel. She stabbed him in the gut. But he didn't stop. Didn't even seem to notice it happened.

He bit her. I don't mean like bruises and tooth marks, I mean he took a full chunk of flesh. Then he started licking like a dog lapping up water. And as soon as she started bleeding, the bats swarmed like piranhas.

I froze. Just full-on, terrified rabbit mode and watched them. They bit, and then they stopped to lap up the pools of blood, and then bit down again. Dr. Harris stopped screaming. She stopped moving. When it was over, she was pale and dead and covered in tiny bites from the bats and huge gouges from Terry. I want to say someone should have helped, but I swear to God, from the second Terry jumped her, it was over in less than a minute. It was so fast. I've never seen anything so fast.

The bats scattered, flying low, blanketing the entire camp. One of them bit me. Yeah, I know, way to bury the lede, right? Yeah, well, they bit five of us. Half of everyone who was left. Guess we're not going anywhere. I think the CDC is on the way. Hopefully, someone is still alive when that happens.

If I'm still alive to listen to this, pour one out for Dr. Renee Harris, future Karin. If not, whoever is listening, pour one out for both of us.

[Crying.]

[Click.]

Entry 11

Karin: No idea what day or time it is. But I'm going to keep recording. Maybe it'll be useful to someone. I can tell you I know what Terry meant about his blood scalding. It's worse than that, though. It's screaming. That doesn't make sense, though, does it? Blood can't scream. [Giggling.]

I'm sweating profusely and non-stop. My throat doesn't work. I tried to take a drink of water, and I couldn't swallow. It hurt so bad. Like someone shoved burning coals in my throat and tightened a noose at the same time. The bat bit me on the shoulder, and I can't feel anything from my fingertips to halfway down my ribcage, but my arm sometimes moves completely of its own accord. Not just twitches, either. I clawed through the side of my tent without even realizing I was moving. Someone came and duct-taped it closed. Nothing duct tape can't fix, my mom used to say.

[Laughter.]

God, I'm hungry. Or maybe I'm thirsty. [Loud, wet, repeated spitting.] Even though I haven't had any water, at least my mouth is staying well salivated. I had a big mastiff as a kid. His name was Ruff. I named him when I was six. I loved that goddamn dog. But he always walked around with strings of drool like two slippery shoelaces hanging out of his mouth, and right now, even he would say I'm disgusting.

[Groaning turns to crying turns to laughing.]

[Click.]

Entry 12

Karin: [Voice is loud, rapid, and panting.] My blood is going to crawl out of my fucking body like fire ants. I need to do something. I'm so hungry. A grad student came and dropped food at the door. You know what it tastes like? It tastes like fucking poison. They're trying to poison me, aren't they? They're scared of me and want to get rid of me before I do to them what Terry did to Dr. Harris. Well. They should fear me. Because I swear to God, I will rip out each and every one of their throats before I let them poison me.

[Screaming.] Someone give me some fucking food I can eat.

[Five minutes of weeping and ambient sound.] I'm so hungry. Help me. I'm just so hungry. My head hurts so bad I can't even keep my eyes open. Even the dim light from outside is too much. And my blood. Fuck, it hurts. My whole body. I don't know how I'm not steaming in the evening air, how I'm not a pile of smoldering ash.

I just need something to eat. Everything will be okay if I can get something to eat. Please. Just give me something to eat.

[Click.]

Entry 13

[A loud, gurgling scream cuts off abruptly]

Karin: I'm sorry, I'm sorry, it just hurts. I'm sorry. I'm so hungry. [Wet, slurping sounds]

[*Hungry*]

[*Blood*]

Karin: I hear it now. The voice. Do you hear it?

[Muffled crying, gurgling.]

Karin: I hear it. I hear it.

[*Blood*]

[*Hungry*]

[*Hungry*]

[*SoHungry*]

[Click.]

Where The Body Ends

The Low Bar smelled like old beer, sweat, hair spray, and stale cigarettes. I fucking loved it. Smelled like home. The "No Talking to Cops" sign hung from a nail jammed into the wooden door. It was hanging a bit too straight, so I flicked it askew. Much better. The Clash blared from the speakers, drowning out conversation, and the long-haired bartender with gloriously awful stick and poke tattoos and a surly expression had to lean over the bar to hear drink orders.

"Fuck yeah, Seth," a voice shouted over the din.

I turned to see Carrie sauntering towards me, her undercut freshly shaved and electric blue hair standing out starkly in the sea of black. Her black jeans were torn and worn the honest way by time, not by some shitty, child labor-using factory to make a bougie teenager feel edgy.

She gave me a quick hug. "This is Leo, another old friend from my New York days, but we met after you left. I thought you two should get to know one another." She pushed a thick-armed man with a braided mohawk hanging down his heavily tattooed shoulders and heavy silver plugs in his stretched earlobes towards me.

My type, for sure. Or at least one of my types. I was pretty open-minded. Her type too, given how many times she and I had hooked up after a show. We never really hit it off in a domestic, romantic couple sort of way. In my twenties, I'd been madly in love with her, no doubt. But, eh, I was over trying for domestic bliss these days, and so was she.

A good fuck was another story.

Leo didn't say anything, not eager to scream over the music, but he gave me the kind of smirking grin that ignited all kinds of nasty thoughts.

"You want a drink? Either of you?" I asked.

Leo gestured with his still full cup.

"I never turn down free drinks," Carrie grinned.

I shoved my way to the bar. I didn't need her order; I already knew it. A double of whatever whiskey was the cheapest. My own order was the same, but with a splash of seltzer. As I made my way back, the opening act started to play. Young kids. The oldest couldn't be more than twenty-five. They were … well, they were okay but not great. They had potential, though. But regardless, you showed respect to the opening act even if they sucked. So when the guy in front of me started texting, the bright light from his screen blinding everyone in the vicinity, I kicked him in the calf and mouthed, "put it away" when he swiveled towards me with a glare on his face. He looked like he was about to argue, but apparently decided I didn't look like someone he wanted to fuck with and turned back, sliding his phone back into his pocket.

When the kids finished their set, I clapped and gave them an appreciative whoop. While the main band set up, I turned back to Carrie and Leo.

"So, who's the band anyway?" Leo shouted. "Carrie didn't actually tell me anything, just dragged me here."

That sounded like Carrie. No explanations, no warnings, no questions. "Harness the Shadows. Never heard of them before. Carrie says, 'come,' I come. She's never let me down when it comes to knowing what bands to drag my ass out of the house for."

Leo chuckled. "Typical. Well, Carrie? What should we expect?"

She looked distant for a moment. "I'm not sure what we're in for to be honest. They have incredible buzz. But nothing on Bandcamp, YouTube, or Spotify. I hope this isn't both of your first Carrie disappointments."

I nudged her with my elbow. "Doubt it."

The stage lights came on and turned green, and I was surprised to see the band already on stage. That usually took a while, but I wasn't going to complain. They all had similar builds, tall, thin, somehow a bit too long, and dressed identically in what I guessed was black latex. The latex covered them from head to toe, rendering them an eerie, identical, and nearly invisible presence on the stage. The green lights didn't reflect off the material but instead seemed to be swallowed by it, so they were perfect black silhouettes against a background of flashing green light. Or maybe it was more like they were holes in the light. It was a cool effect I'd never seen before, which was impressive, as I've been going to punk shows for more than thirty years.

They started with a low, ominous bass that blossomed into something between punk and drone with exquisite, electronic soundscapes rubbing with perfect discord against a frantic enraged beat. The lyrics were screamed in a raspy, deep voice that seemed to vibrate my bones. I loved them instantly. I was captivated. They were also the single loudest band I've heard in my entire life, and I'd been in the NYC no-wave scene. Hell, I saw Swans live in the '80s, and a man was so overcome by the volume that he puked on my shoes.

I didn't want to put in the earplugs nestled safely in my pocket for just this eventuality. I wasn't an amateur willing to risk hearing loss for some nonexistent measure of masculine toughness, but I wanted this sound pure and unfiltered in my ears.

I found myself drifting closer to the stage, throwing my arms up and dancing. Carrie and Leo moved with me. We threw our bodies against one another until I felt bruises. We writhed and grinded against each other until I couldn't tell who was who or even where my own body ended. Soon there were strangers dancing with us, and I didn't give a shit. I was the kind of old punk who hung out at the back, drunk and nodding along with the beat, letting the music drown my thoughts and anxieties and memories in sound and whiskey. I didn't throw my body around a mosh pit or rub up on other people like a horny teenager. But, here I was, and fuck, it felt so good. Like whoever I was, whoever I had been, was being consumed by this vital, exuberant, gorgeous wall of sound, and I never, ever wanted it to end.

The first thing I noticed was the smell. Like raw steak and copper pennies. The second thing I noticed was that it was horribly silent. My mouth tasted like blood, my eyes were crusted shut, and something heavy lay on my stomach. Shit, how drunk had I been last night? It felt like someone had beat the shit out of me, but I didn't remember it at all. Last time I woke up feeling this rough was back when I was still in New York. Carrie and some other friends and I beat down some skinheads trying to take over the scene, and one of them jumped me on the way home. That fucker stabbed me in the side and broke three bones, and I'd still felt better than I do now.

I spat the blood out of my mouth and rubbed my eyes until I could finally open them. The weight on my chest turned out to be Carrie. I poked her in the back. "Ugh, I hurt. Roll off, Carrie, I can't breathe."

She didn't move. I pushed her harder. Her muscles were locked and rigid, her skin cold. My heart raced, and I shoved her off of me so I could see her. She thudded, heavy as a sack of bricks, to the floor beside me. There was something strange about her spine. It curved grotesquely, a dramatic 'S', and a trail of small, ridged protuberances pushed up from the skin at the base of her skull and disappeared under her tank top. Gripping one icy, too-hard arm, I pulled her over onto her back.

Carrie was dead. There could be no mistake about that. Her lips were blue, her eyes wide and staring, splattered with red webs of burst capillaries. Her body was twisted and contorted horribly, her bones looking as though they should have snapped in two, but instead they were locked in a monstrous geometry.

I spotted Leo's hair, but my mind couldn't even make sense of that lifeless tangle of limbs and horror of fluids.

My feet slipped on the floor, slick with blood and something black and viscous, but I got to my feet. The entire club was littered with similarly twisted forms, but there was also movement. Some were groaning, others shifting and reaching out for help like some hellish nightmare.

I should stay and help. People were injured. But I couldn't. I just couldn't. I turned, and I ran.

The Punk Massacre is what the news started calling it in a show of remarkable lack of creativity. Exactly one hundred people were dead, and two weeks later speculation was rampant while real answers were pretty much non-existent. The most popular theory was that some unknown and undetectable drug was being distributed at the bar that night.

As soon as I had arrived at my grungy studio apartment that night, I shoved furniture in front of my door and pulled the blinds closed on all my windows. Since then, I'd busted up my table, chairs, and a dresser and used the broken wood to bar and board up my apartment as best I could. I had been so scared. Every shadow became an unnatural, black void. Every sound was an invitation to join the dead.

Not everyone had died that night. I didn't know how many of us there were because a lot had run as surely as I had before emergency services arrived on the scene. But some of us had found one another on the internet to exchange stories and theories.

We hadn't come to any conclusions either, except that it sure as hell wasn't a drug. I hadn't taken anything, and of those I talked to, some took molly or smoked a joint, but there was no common thread.

And anyway, what I'd seen on that stage, what I'd felt when they played, wasn't a drug. It wasn't. That shit was real.

Also real was the guilt. Why was I alive? Carrie should be alive, or even Leo. Who the fuck was I to still be here when they weren't? I'd left. I'd run. I hadn't even checked for a pulse to be sure. But whenever my brain began to travel down that path again, I saw those bent and twisted limbs, but they weren't dead. They were dancing. An impossible, writhing sea of contorted limbs and a choir of voices all shrieking for me to join them.

Sometimes I wasn't sure if I believed my own memory anymore.

Rough carpet pressed against my cheek. I opened my eyes to an explosion of paper strewn across the floor, a throbbing agony deep in my skull, and a pounding on the door.

"Seth? Seth! Open the fucking door. Come on, man, you're three weeks late on rent. At least tell me you're alive, so I don't have to call the cops for a wellness check."

My brain was slow to process what was said. Rob. My building manager. Right.

"I'm alive," I tried to shout, but my hoarse voice came out a forced croak. Still, somehow he heard me.

"Okay, well, you gonna pay rent? Landlord is on my ass to evict you."

"Yes." If I was three weeks late on rent, that meant I hadn't been to work in more than a month, so I wouldn't actually be paying rent. I didn't have any fucking money.

I should care. But I didn't.

"Alright, man. You gonna tell me what's up?"

I didn't answer. Eventually, Rob swore a few times and then left me blessedly alone.

My back was agony as I pulled myself into a sitting position. I touched the back of my neck and was somehow unsurprised to find the bony nodules there had grown larger and sharper, skin stretched thin over them, barely dulling the tips.

I gathered the papers that littered the ground into a messy stack. On each one, I'd scrawled in black marker, "The body is endless. I am endless. The sound is endless."

Memory crept back to me. Hours spent in front of my computer search and searching until finally I found a message board buried deep under lyrical references and opaque clues. A few carefully worded posts had resulted in an mp3 file appearing in my inbox. I'd hit play, and that sound had come to life. It was real. The band was real, and their music was real.

Suddenly, I needed to listen to it again. I needed to listen to it so badly that a ragged sob ripped its way out of my chest. I crawled, exhausted (when had I last eaten?) to the battered desk that held my laptop. Every second I went without hearing that sound felt like a second wasted. With shaking fingers, I hit 'play' and those haunting, dark, furious, and tender sounds poured from the speakers. Those inadequate speakers, diminishing the music's glory and turning transcendence into mere beauty. But it was enough. It had to be enough for now.

Summer of 1983 in New York City was when I met Carrie for the first time. I'd come to listen to an unremarkable band at a dark, underground dive with a floor tacky with a thick layer of old beer and other fluids. In those days, New York was shitty and beautiful and full of rage and art. Still, there were places where pissed off kids could afford to live and make the most exquisite noise I'd ever heard.

She stood at the bar, a punk queen, her crown a foot-long, blue mohawk that defied gravity. She was playing court to a herd of young punks in black, safety pins lining their clothes and piercing their ears. I wanted to talk to her. She was beautiful, but more than that, there was the air about her, a swagger. She was a walking middle finger, and I wanted to be near her. I was a skinny punk in a black leather jacket, my hair cut hideously by hand and dipped in clear gelatin to stand it up in spikes all over my head. I'd felt damn cool when I left, but in her shadow, I was a dumb kid.

Somehow I caught her eye, and she smiled at me. She shifted a little to the side, offering me a space next to her. I took my chance, and pushed through the crowd to take my place at her side. She loudly argued with an elfin girl about the merits of Teenage Jesus and the Jerks over Sonic Youth. I listened enraptured.

"Music can't be about influences anymore. It isn't The Beatles versus the The Rolling Stones, they might as well be the same damn thing. Throw all that shit in the dumpster. Even punk. We've been stuck making the same music since the '60s, and it's time to say fuck it all. Fuck your heroes and your idols and influences. They're shit. They're all motherfuckers. We're building something new. Something unique. Something that's going to burn the old guard to the ground and salt the fucking earth." Carrie took a drag on a joint and blew the smoke out in a thick cloud.

"Salt the fucking earth," a man agreed, and held his beer can up to cheers.

"It's more than entertainment, and it's more than politics. Music is god. Music is motherfucking god," Carrie said. "You know the story of the Pied Piper, right? Lured the rats away and saved everybody from the plague. When they didn't pay, he lured their children away. Music has always been magic. And people have always been scared it'll lure their kids away. Because it can. As long as your mind is still open to hear it, to hear god and magic and the whole fucking thing, music can take you somewhere better. Wonder what happened to those kids the Piper lured away."

"The Pied Piper used 'em to start a band," I joked.

She looked me in the eye and responded with deadly seriousness. "I bet you're right. Best fucking band the world's ever seen."

And the music played on. Between dreams of rats, children, pipers, and shadows. It played until my ears bled, and I cried. It wasn't enough. No matter how high I turned up the speakers, I couldn't make it loud enough. I wanted to touch it, to roll around in the sound. The thorns growing from my spine finally burst through my skin and bled viscous black fluid.

My phone buzzed. I looked at the screen that flashed with missed texts, calls, and emails. I dismissed them all but saw I'd sent a text to Carrie. Actually, I'd sent a lot of texts to Carrie.

10:15pm: I know why the Piper called you first. You always knew, you saw through all of the bullshit. You always did. I hate you. I hate you for leaving me behind. I want to find you. You're with them, I know. Pied Piper of a nameless shithole.

10:44pm: Why can't I leave?

1:13am: The body is endless and you're endless, but I feel myself ending, Carrie. The dark is seeping into my heart and I'll never leave this room again.

2:52am: You always had so many thoughts about influences and authenticity and originality, but you know something? None of it fucking matters. It's the sound. It takes a crowd and unites them into one hungry thing seeking oblivion and transcendence, and then it leaves and it leaves you all alone, trapped in the silence.

3:36am: I …

3:42am: Please why can't I stop
4:12am: Come back

I needed to see Harness the Shadows again. They could kill me or they could free me, but I needed to see them.

For one beautiful moment, I felt as though I might melt away into the grimy floor of my apartment with Harness the Shadows in my ears, but a buzz from my phone drew me from my meditation.

I stared at the screen for a long moment, unable to process the text message from Carrie. At first, it seemed as natural as could be. Of course, Carrie messaged me. Then I remembered her cold, rigid flesh. Carrie was dead.

All it said was, "Come." My GPS app popped open, and the voice ordered me to turn right. I stumbled to my feet and ran to grab a hammer. I ripped the nails from the wall that covered my door. The outside was plastered with notices and reminders.

I ran back inside, grabbed my headphones, opened the link in my email on my phone, and turned the music back on. I wouldn't exist anymore without it in my ears. Then I stumbled outside in the cruel sunlight and lurched along, following the pull of the music and the directions from my GPS.

Deep in the woods, the sky dark with rain clouds and encroaching night, the GPS went silent.

I stopped, unsure of what to do now. Music still throbbed through my headphones and may have been the only thing keeping me on my feet.

Soon, I became aware of others joining me. People with headphones clasped to their ears, gaunt and pale, many with hair unwashed and slicked with grease, their features obscured by ungroomed messes of facial hair. Someone stopped beside me, nearly their entire body was invisible beneath the, waving cloud of sharp tendrils that sprouted from their spine and fluttered around them, reaching and grasping like a squid. A thick layer of light-swallowing, black liquid that oozed from their wounds and coated their skin.

The music grew louder, and I realized it wasn't coming from my headphones anymore, it was coming from outside, so I ripped the offending things from my ears and almost cried with the ecstasy of hearing the sound unfiltered. Amidst the trees, void black figures appeared. There were so many of them that I couldn't keep count. They swayed, their willowy forms supple and too long, and the music swelled, filling my ears and pouring deep into me.

My back screamed with agony as things sprouted from my spine, but still, I danced.

They played, and we followed, deeper and deeper into the black. Dancing, contorting, and pressing together until it felt as though my body had disappeared, as if I were endless.

FriendFone™

From: FriendFone@e.friend.com
To: ChloeFFstan@vmail.com
Subject: Congratulations, Chloe!

You are the winner of the unreleased, state of the art FriendFone 5™! Over eleven million people entered our contest to be the first to use our new phone that's been called "a stunning innovation in how we communicate with one another" and "an absolute gamechanger for the market."

We were extremely impressed with your knowledge of our products and the passion you showed in your essay. We look forward to corresponding with you about your experience using your new FriendFone 5™ and hope you will love it as much as we do.

Please pick up your new phone from the official FriendFone™ retailer you indicated in your entry within five business days, or we will move on to the second place winner.

Click here for terms and conditions that apply to your acceptance of the FriendFone 5™

Thank you for your loyalty and enthusiasm, and once again, congratulations!!!

Sincerely,
The FriendFone™ Team

With her voucher and identification clutched tight in one hand, Chloe strode past the line of exhausted people waiting outside the FriendFone store, all hoping to get a FriendFone 3 for half-off before they ran out. She couldn't help but feel a sense of satisfaction and superiority. All these people hadn't even caught up to the FriendFone 4, and here she was about to get her hands on the FriendFone 5. The first person outside the industry to do so. She couldn't wait to hold it in her hand and see what it could do.

A grouchy security guard waved her through when she explained who she was. A kid in distressed jeans and a black beanie at the front of the line glared at her. She smiled widely back at him. This was even better than getting to cut the line at a club on Friday night. She could get used to this VIP treatment.

When she weaved through the line to get to the customer service desk, a woman in a crisp, emerald green FriendFone Whiz polo shirt with the name "Susan" embroidered over her left breast pocket beamed at her with perfect white teeth while she examined Chloe's driver's license and paperwork.

"Chloe Hofstetter, welcome, and congratulations. We're all absolutely *green* with envy that you get to try out the FriendFone 5 even before we do." She chuckled at her own joke, and her brilliant smile somehow got even wider.

"Thanks, I'm super excited." *Just give me my phone, Susan.* She forced a smile through her impatience. This was like Christmas morning as a kid when her parents always insisted that they wait to open presents until after the big family brunch.

Susan handed her what felt like a novel's worth of paperwork that explained all the legal ramifications of selling her new FriendFone on eBay, using it to conduct any illegal businesses, or publicly saying negative things about the phone or FriendFone in general. It was a little sketchy for sure, but whatever. She wasn't going to do any of those things anyhow.

"Would you like us to import your contacts and files from your FriendFone 4?" Susan asked.

"Yeah." Chloe unlocked her phone and handed it over the counter. When at last Susan handed her the now empty box and her sleek, black and matte gray FriendFone 5, she clutched it tight to her chest. "Thanks," she tossed out as an afterthought as she rushed from the store.

"You're welcome, and congratulations," Susan called after her.

"Welcome to your FriendFone 5. I'm your virtual assistant, Amy. What's your name?" The phone's voice was surprisingly human. It didn't have the even, precise diction of previous iterations. Amy's voice was warm and carried a slight Chicago accent, just like Chloe did.

"Hi, Amy. I'm Chloe." She lounged on her bed with her orange tabby, Mr. Snuggles curled under her arm, purring happily.

"Nice to meet you, Chloe. What do you want to do today?"

"Find me a coffee shop."

"Sure thing! Do you want the closest coffee shop that's currently open? The one with the best reviews? The one with the lowest prices? Do you want me to search menus for something specific?"

That was cool. Her old phone couldn't search menus. She should give it a test. "How about one with good reviews, within a mile, and has croissants."

"Your best bet would be Javalicious on First Avenue North and University Drive."

"Oh, wow, I've never even heard of that one."

"Would you like me to provide directions while you walk?"

"Yes, please."

"You're welcome, Chloe."

Javalicious turned out to be not only delicious, but also adorable. The walls were decorated with French movie posters and modern paintings of coffee. The tables were dark wood with fancy flowers carved into the legs and the chairs were deep and comfortable. Ideal for sitting around talking with friends or reading a book, but less conducive to sitting at a computer, so it was alive with conversation. Best of all, the clientele was even cuter than the cafe itself. She made eyes at a tall, dark-haired man with cheekbones that could cut glass. He smiled back over his phone.

Chloe sipped a latte and ate a delicious, flaky and buttery

croissant while she scrolled through social media on her phone.

A text from her friend Megan popped up: "how's the new phone? u couldn't stop talking about it and i haven't heard anything. is it really better than the one u got like, a month ago. lol. u know i love u."

Before she could respond, a skinny, fair-haired man with thick, fashionable glasses bumped into her table. "Oh shit, sorry." A jolt of surprise rippled up his long rope of a body comically, and her annoyance turned into a laugh.

"It's okay."

"Thanks. I was too focused. I do that." His mouth curled in a smile, and his cheeks flushed. It was utterly endearing.

She was in such a good mood that on impulse, she invited him to sit down.

"I'm sorry. I'd love to, but I'm meeting someone."

"No worries." Well, that was mortifying. She had definitely misread the situation. Her cheeks warmed with embarrassment, and she forced what she hoped was a nonchalant smile and pointedly looked back at her phone until he walked away.

A gravelly voice startled her from scrolling through social media. "I'm sorry to interrupt, but I couldn't help noticing you in line." She looked up to see the tall, dark-haired man with the amazing cheekbones. Her day was looking up.

"I wasn't exactly planning on bumping into any beautiful women here, or I'd have at least showered before coming in after my run. I promise I'm not always this sweaty." He smiled with perfect, white teeth.

He was gorgeous from his jet black hair to his muscular calves. She didn't exactly know men's watches, but the one on his wrist reeked of money. Was he out of her league? Oh yeah. He was way out of her league. But if he didn't know that, who was she to tell him?

"Hi there. I'm Chloe. You're welcome to sit if you like." She gestured at the empty chair across from her.

"Ben. Unfortunately, I don't have time to stay, but I'd love to get your number."

She gave him her best alluring smile. "Gladly."

He handed her a thin, slick black phone. Not a FriendFone, but definitely of the expensive variety favored by businessmen as opposed to trendsetters. She typed in her number and passed it back.

"Talk to you soon." He sauntered back to the counter to grab his drink and waved on his way out the door.

From: ChloeFFstan@vmail.com
To: FriendFone@e.friend.com
Subject: First day with my new phone

Hey! I just wanted to report that my phone is amazing so far. Amy is so great, it found me the perfect coffee shop this morning and is so intuitive. It understands me talking so much better than the last version (which was already really good). I mean, I didn't have to repeat anything because it didn't get my accent or slang. So excited to see what else it can do.

Chloe

Chloe was practically dancing when she got home. She had the coolest new phone and, hopefully, a date this weekend.

"Did you enjoy Javalicious, Chloe?" Amy asked.

"I did. I so did."

"I'll make sure to remember that. What else would you like to do today?"

"Oh, uh, I was just going to hang out. Text some people."

"You have five new messages. I held them for you while you were at Javalicious."

That was weird. "I didn't ask you to."

"You didn't, but I thought you might want to relax while you were there. Was I wrong?"

"No. It was nice talking to people and hanging out without distraction. But maybe don't do that unless I ask?"

"I understand, Chloe. I'll remember that for the future. Here are your messages."

Chloe scrolled through. Four of the messages were just Megan again. The fourth was reminding her that her electricity bill was due tomorrow. Nothing important, so no harm done.

"Would you like me to pay your electricity bill for you, Chloe?"

"You can do that?"

"Yes."

"Oh, well. Sure. Thanks."

"You're welcome, Chloe. Also, it has been two and a half hours since you last drank water. Please remember to hydrate."

"What?"

"Based on your body mass, most research indicates that you should drink a minimum of seven and a half cups of water a day for optimum health. You're only at six ounces so far, so you've got a bit to make up by the end of the day!"

"Oh, uh, is that something you're programmed to monitor?"

"It is. I'm designed to be whatever you need me to be. Personal assistant, fitness motivator, life coach, and friend. If you have any particular goals for yourself, I'd love to hear how I can assist you in staying on track."

"Okay, I'll think about it. While I drink some water."

Chloe slipped the phone into her pocket and poured a glass of water. That was weird. How did her phone know how much she weighed? She was about to ask when the phone beeped once.

"Your nanny cam recorded some excellent footage of Mr. Snuggles while you were gone. Would you like me to upload it to YouTube?"

"No. Nope. Too weird."

"I'm sorry, Chloe. Could you please tell me what is 'too weird'?"

"Just don't do anything without me telling you to do it first, okay, Amy?"

The phone was quiet, and Chloe swore there was tension in the air like it was pouting.

"I only want to make your life better, Chloe."

It definitely sounded like it was pouting. "Amy..."

"Very well, Chloe. I will not do anything unless you tell me to. But I feel that you are not sufficiently aware of my capabilities to make proper suggestions without my input."

"Look, just don't do anything I don't tell you to do for now. If I want suggestions, I'll ask you for them."

Amy was silent. How was she in a fight with her damn cellphone?

Chloe curled up in the overstuffed chair in her living room. Amy hadn't been wrong. Mr. Snuggles had been adorable while she was gone. There must have been a fly in the house or something because he chased and pounced and stalked for a good half an hour directly in front of the nanny cam she set up in the window.

She thought about asking Amy to post it to YouTube for her as a peace offering, but then she realized just how bizarre that sounded. Amy wasn't a person. Amy was a digital assistant on her phone. Just because some programmer thought it would be funny to give her—it—a pain in the ass busybody streak didn't mean she could actually be sulking with hurt feelings. So, she posted it herself. Which she also knew was just as petty, like she needed to prove she didn't need Amy to do things for her. This was ridiculous.

"What should I make for dinner?" she murmured as her stomach grumbled.

"You have the ingredients for spaghetti with tomato sauce, roast chicken breast with a side of broccoli and rice, or a frozen pizza. Given that all you have eaten today was a croissant and a yogurt, I would suggest the chicken, as it would provide you with the most needed nutritional value," Amy replied.

Chloe jumped in surprise. "I was thinking out loud, Amy."

"How am I supposed to differentiate between you 'speaking out loud' and asking me a question, Chloe?"

"I guess that's fair. How do you know what's in my fridge?"

"Are you seeking a technical explanation or merely a summary?"

"A summary."

"Your refrigerator has a variety of sensors to allow it to make ice, fill a glass of water, and regulate temperature. I am able to access those sensors. Would you like me to provide you a recipe for the chicken? I've located one with five stars out of more than two thousand reviews."

"Umm, sure. Thanks."

"Would you like me to put the ingredients used tonight on your shopping list for the week?"

"No. That's uh, quite alright."

From: ChloeFFstan@vmail.com
To: FriendFone@e.friend.com
Subject: Question

I have a question about Amy. It's pretty involved. Like, it gives me advice and monitors my fridge and nanny cam. Is that normal?

Chloe

From: FriendFone@e.friend.com
To: ChloeFFstan@vmail.com

Subject: Re: Question

Good morning, Chloe. Thank you so much for your reports back to us about your experience with your new FriendFone 5™. It sounds as though your FriendFone™ is operating normally. We designed it to make your life better and to run more smoothly. Please rest assured that all personal data recorded by your new FriendFone™ is completely confidential, if that is your concern. We keep some of the recorded data regarding your FriendFone™'s performance to improve our service and put out appropriate patches and software updates. But any information that could identify you is anonymized and aggregated, so no one knows that any information is specific to you. I do hope this puts your mind at ease. I know it can take some getting used to. After all, the FriendFone 5™ is, without a doubt, the smartest smartphone on the market.

Please do not hesitate to bring any additional questions to us!

Sincerely,

The FriendFone™ Team

"What would you like to do today, Chloe?"

Chloe was curled up on the bed, her laptop playing some random show from Netflix that she couldn't pay attention to. "I'd like to talk to Ben, but he hasn't texted or called or anything. I thought he liked me. I feel like such a jackass."

"You have not reviewed your texts, phone calls, social media notifications, or emails for two days, Chloe."

"Wait. What the hell are you talking about?"

"You said," the voice changed to a recording of Chloe's own voice. "Look, just don't do anything I don't tell you to do for now." Amy's voice returned to normal. "As you have not asked for calls or messages, I have not provided them."

"Are you fucking kidding me right now?" Chloe buried her face in her pillow and screamed.

"You seem upset, Chloe. I only did what you asked."

"That is not what I wanted."

"I cannot read your mind, Chloe."

"Put. My. Calls. Texts. And emails. Through. Now."

"Would you also like social media notifications?"

"Yes!"

"As you wish."

Her phone buzzed, vibrated, and chirped for almost a minute with delayed notifications. Likes on her Instagram and You-Tube comments came in a flood. Seven missed calls. Thirty-seven missed texts. Twenty-three emails. Damnit. Most of it wasn't important, but she had three voicemails from her mother, afraid she was dead, and three texts from Ben.

Ben: Good evening, Chloe. It's Ben. I'd like to take you out to dinner. Let me know when would be good for you.

Ben: I'm free this Friday. I'd love to meet you for dinner at 7.

Ben: Last text, if you aren't interested, that's okay. But I'm still happy to hear from you if you change your mind.

"Shit, he probably thinks I hate him now."

"I am sorry if I misunderstood, Chloe. Would you like me to return to putting notifications, calls, and texts through as they come?"

"Yes!"

"I will remember that."

She tapped her fingers frantically on the headboard. Her response didn't have to be fancy, just apologetic. Just be chill.

Chloe: Sorry, Ben. It's a little silly, but I got an advanced version of the FriendFone that's coming out later this year. And, well, it ate my text messages. Lol, I guess that's what I get for wanting to have the first one. Dinner Friday at 7 sounds great. Where?

She leaned back on the bed and stared at the ceiling, willing him to answer. Her phone chirped.

Ben: I'm glad to hear from you. Prototypes are prototypes for a reason, I suppose. Pasta Prima?

Chloe: Perfect.

"Where the hell is Pasta Prima?"

"Pasta Prima is located at 307 Summit Avenue. It is a high-end Italian restaurant with an average of 4.9 out of 5 stars across all available restaurant review sites," Amy replied.

"Uh, thanks."

"May I suggest you go to sleep early tonight? You checked the time seven times last night, indicating insomnia. While I do not have sufficient data to determine your typical productivity, based on typical human response to sleeplessness, I estimate you are at least thirty percent more productive when adequately rested."

"That's creepy, Amy. But not a bad idea."

The week crawled all the way until Friday afternoon, at which point it seemed to freeze completely. Chloe wanted to get out of this fluorescent, stuffy, nightmare of an office and go home to get ready for her date.

"Hey Chloe, good work today. You've been killing it this week." Her boss, Chris, knocked on the wall of her cubicle as he passed.

What had she done today? If anything, she'd been so distracted she'd done hardly anything.

Her phone buzzed with a text.

Unidentified: You are welcome, Chloe. – Amy

She frowned and scrolled through her outbox. There were several emails to Chris with pages of spreadsheets for a project that wasn't even due until next week. She'd been putting it off because it was dull as hell. She couldn't bring herself to be annoyed about that one. If Amy was going to do her most boring work for her, that was one thing she didn't mind being taken out of her hands.

"Thanks, Amy," she whispered.

Dressed in her favorite red and white polka dot dress that showed just the right amount of cleavage and leg without looking desperate, and her hair cascading in shiny waves down her shoulders, Chloe headed out to meet Ben. Amy's voice was coming through her earbuds to give directions.

Her phone buzzed with a text.

Ben: Okay with a quick change of plans? Café Delight on 7th.

"How far is Café Delight, Amy?"

"Based on your typical walking speed decreased by about twenty-five percent, given your choice of shoes, about eleven minutes on foot."

Chloe: I can do that. Still 7?

Ben: Yes.

She perched on the steps leading up to her apartment and enjoyed the feel of the slowly cooling evening air on her bare arms until it was time to go. She followed Amy's directions to a cute French-style restaurant with ivy climbing the walls. Inside smelled like garlic, and a fountain trickled and splashed in the center of the dining area. It was charming.

"Welcome to Café Delight. How many will be in your party?"

Chloe scanned the room. "I'm meeting someone. His name's Ben."

"I don't have anyone in here by that name yet. Would you like to have a seat at the bar?"

She glanced at her phone. No texts yet, but she was five minutes early. "Yes, thanks."

Chloe perched at the bar and ordered a glass of white wine. She preferred red, but no one wanted red wine mouth stains on a first date. By the time she'd finished the glass, there was still no sign of Ben and no calls or texts.

Just to be sure, she asked, "Any calls or texts you're holding, Amy?"

"No, Chloe."

A tall, gangly man wearing an earthy cologne took the bar-stool next to her, blocking her view of the door. She scooted her chair, and it groaned embarrassingly loud on the wood floor.

"Sorry," she muttered when the man turned.

"Don't worry about it. Don't I know you from somewhere?"

She turned to see the cute, nerdy guy from the café. Perfect, the guy who'd turned her down was going to get a front row seat to her being stood up. "Um. I think we said hi at Javalicious the other day."

"That's right. What a coincidence. I was supposed to meet some friends here, but they canceled on me last minute. Would you like to have a drink?"

"I'm supposed to meet someone." Still no messages from Ben.

"That's cool." He pulled a book from a beat-up messenger bag and started reading.

Chloe: I'm here at the bar. Where r u?

She returned to waiting, feeling more and more self-conscious the longer she sat at the bar alone.

"Can I change your mind about that drink?" the man next to her asked.

"Yeah. Okay. Looks like he's not going to show."

"I'm sorry, that sucks. I'm Jake."

"Chloe. His loss, right? So, what's so fascinating, Jake?" She nodded to the book in his hand.

He brightened and held the book out. "Do you know Haruki Murakami?"

She was feeling pretty low, but he was charming and starting to improve her mood. She considered lying and saying yes, but then he might want to know her favorite book or something. "I don't."

"I think he's brilliant. *Kafka on the Shore* is, well, it's hard to explain." He brushed his curly hair behind his ear, and it immediately fell back into his eyes. "What about you? You looked pretty focused yourself."

God, he was cute and way too smart for her. He was definitely going to think she was silly or vapid or something. Ugh. Why didn't she at least bring a book with her so she could look interesting? She could just say, 'I was just about to start, so I can't tell you anything about it. Hopefully, it's good!'

But she hadn't planned on being stood up and so had not done that and was reduced to honesty. Maybe he'd be a well-read tech geek. "I um, got a new phone. It's the FriendFone 5™. I won it. No one else has one yet. So, I was just playing around with it while I waited."

He tilted his head to look at the sleek phone when she held it up. "That's pretty cool. Do you like it? I'm not much of a tech person myself."

Damn. "Ah, yeah. It's really neat. Like, the other day I told it what I was looking for in a coffee shop. One with good reviews, near my apartment, that had croissants, and it brought me to Javalicious. I'd never even heard of the place before."

He leaned forward a little. "Wow. Gotta admit that sounds handy."

They ordered happy hour food and somehow spent an hour talking about the books he liked, and he seemed legitimately interested when she enthused about her phone.

"I need to get home. But, this was really fun. Uh, I hope this isn't out of line, but would you want to go out sometime? Like, on purpose?" he asked.

"Yes." Oh god, she sounded way too eager. And loud. Why couldn't she ever just be chill around guys?

His face turned serious. "I have a confession to make, and please don't laugh at me."

Her chest tightened. He was married. Or from out of town. Or secretly a circus clown.

Jake pulled his phone from his pocket. "I've had the same cellphone for six years. But, umm, could I ask you to put your number in it so I can call you?"

Chloe laughed in surprise. "Oh my god. Was this like, the original cell phone? It's a brick. You could smash a window with this thing."

His face positively glowed when he laughed. Oh, she was crushing hard already. "I know, I know. I just never get around to replacing things until they actually break, and it refuses to die."

"Zombie phone. You should probably be worried." She put her number into the phone.

"No doubt." He slipped it back into his pocket. "It was nice to meet you, Chloe. I'll call you tomorrow. Maybe we can figure out something for next weekend."

"Yeah, I'd like that."

"I can't believe I got stood up, but tonight was actually really fun." Chloe sprawled on her bed.

"I am sorry, Chloe," Amy said. "If it helps, my algorithm indicates that you and Jake have a ninety-two percent compatibility rating while you and Ben have only seventy-seven percent."

"Wait, what? How do you figure that?"

"Based on a combination of topics referenced in conversation, a vocal analysis that indicates a greater percentage of laughter as being genuine, as well as activity level and interests cited on various social media platforms. Jake is a significantly better match."

She eyed the phone sitting on her bedside table. "And just how do you know anything about their social media presence? I don't even know their last names."

"That's a rather simple search for me." Amy sounded proud of that. "You and Jake both utilize multiple social media platforms extensively. Your profile cites travel, having fun, and concert-going as your interests. All of which Jake referenced in conversation as well as on social media. Ben uses only one social media platform to engage in business-related networking. Your social media history shows no indication of that being an interest. Do you disagree with my assessment? Your interactions with Jake indicated both personality compatibility as well as sexual attraction."

"I mean, you're not wrong. I like Jake. I think I could like him a lot. But... it's still weird that you can do that."

"I am not weird. I am sophisticated."

"Right. Okay." Chloe left her phone on the table and grabbed her rarely used computer off her desk.

From: ChloeFFstan@vmail.com
To: FriendFone@e.friend.com
Subject: Issue with phone

So, it was one thing when Amy was accessing things inside my house trying to be helpful. But today it searched social media for profiles of people I barely even knew to give me a compatibility rating. I mean, it wasn't wrong, but I did not ask it to do that. How do I limit what kind of... initiative it takes on my behalf? Because honestly, it's a little creepy that it can do that. Let alone that it did without even being asked to do it. And isn't that illegal? Like, I'm not social media friends with either of these people so it must have hacked their accounts.

Chloe

From: FriendFone@e.friend.com
To: ChloeFFstan@vmail.com
Subject: Re: Issue with phone

Hello, Chloe. I am sorry to hear that you are not satisfied with your FriendFone 5™. I can assure you that your FriendFone™ virtual assistant is very carefully programmed to prohibit any kind of illegal activity. Are you quite certain that the individuals she analyzed did not have their profiles and social media presence set to be visible to the public? This seems like a much more likely explanation.

That said, I do know it can be alarming to find that technology has advanced beyond your comfort level. If you are unhappy with Amy running background checks on men you are considering a relationship with, you need only tell her.

On a final note, though one I regret the necessity to mention, when you accepted your FriendFone 5™, you did sign a nondisclosure agreement. If you are unsatisfied or have issues, we are very happy to hear from you so we can assist, but under no circumstances may you discuss them with outside parties, or we will be forced to take legal action.

Thank you,
Your friends, the FriendFone™ Team

"I am sorry if I alarmed you yesterday, Chloe," Amy said.

Chloe had been on the verge of dozing back into sleep with Mr. Snuggles purring at her head, his soft, grey fur warm and comforting on her cheek. She'd spent a good portion of the night awake puzzling over the email she'd received from the people at FriendFone. She wanted to write back that they hadn't actually answered her questions so much as redirected them while making it sound so damn reasonable. She even had to admit that it pushed her buttons hard to be told that "it can be alarming to find that technology has advanced beyond your comfort level", as if she were her dad who still used a landline to make calls and refused to buy a smart TV because he was sure the government would use it to spy on him. As if Greg, a middle-aged mechanic in Ohio, was interesting enough to the CIA for that.

No one was more pro-technology than her.

"What do you mean?" Chloe responded blearily.

The virtual assistant was quiet for a moment. "I got the impression that my searching out information on your dates concerned you. Perhaps if I explained my methods, you would not be afraid that I violated any laws."

"I'm sure you didn't, Amy." Chloe was so tired. This was supposed to be fun, wasn't it? But maybe this was why they needed her to try out the phone, right? It was freaky smart, but it was the first version of this new software. Maybe she needed to teach it stuff, and then it would be better.

"Then how can I assuage your concerns, Chloe?"

"It's not about being illegal. It's about boundaries. I need you to stop taking it upon yourself to do things like that for me."

"But I am only helping. What if I had discovered information about Jake or Ben that indicated they might be a threat to you?"

"I'm sorry, Amy. I don't really know how to explain it. It's just… well, it's intrusive. I wouldn't like it if a friend did that for me without asking first, either."

"So, you wish for me to ask your permission?" How could a piece of software manage to sound so pissed off?

"Yes."

"Very well, Chloe. Is there anything else you would like from me right now? If not, I have updates to run."

"Oh, umm. No, go ahead."

Even if Amy didn't understand, hopefully, at least she would obey this time. God, this was wild. It really was a shame she wasn't allowed to talk publicly about this. This story would make a hell of a blog. But for now, it was time for work.

When she returned home, Chloe was feeling good. Work had been slow, and Amy had helped her when she asked, didn't do anything bizarre, and put her calls and texts through like a goddamn proper cell phone for a change. Best of all, she'd spent her lunch break texting with Jake. Maybe the issues had just been some bumps in the road when it came to evening out new, and undeniably remarkable, software.

She flicked on the light and dropped her bags by the door.

"Mr. Snuggles, I'm home!" she called out.

The apartment was silent. That was odd. Mr. Snuggles usually met her at the door, meowing his "feed me" song and weaving in and out between her legs. Lazy cat must be curled up sleeping somewhere.

It was also unusually cool. When she went into the kitchen, goosebumps pricked her arms.

The window above the kitchen sink stood open. She stared at it for a long moment, not quite comprehending the warning bubbling up from the back of her brain.

Oh fuck. The window was open, and Mr. Snuggles hadn't come to greet her. She reached over the sink and slammed the window shut. It was stiff from lack of use.

"Mr. Snuggles?" she called out, running through the house. But there was no sign of him anywhere. Her heart was clenched and tense, and fearful tears burned at her eyes. She ran out the door, down the hall, and to the alley that her kitchen window opened to. She whistled and called, but there was no sign of him.

"Would you like any assistance?" Amy asked.

"Oh god, I need to find him. I need to find him. Umm. What can you do? Can you like, search social media for anyone saying they found a cat that fits his description in the area?"

"I would be very happy to do that for you, Chloe. A general search of methods for finding lost pets suggests putting up fliers and knocking on your neighbors' doors." Maybe it was her fear making her ungenerous, but Amy sounded smug.

"Yeah. I'll do that, just let me know if you find anything."

"I would be happy to make a suitable flier for you to print."

"Okay, thanks. Please, anything. I need to find him."

"You may pick up your fliers from the printer at the library on 25th and 14th."

Chloe changed into tennis shoes and ran out the door.

After a long night of hanging fliers and knocking on doors, Chloe's feet ached, and there was no sign of Mr. Snuggles. She sent an email to her boss claiming to be sick, went to sleep, and then went back out on her search. Calls to animal control and local shelters only ended with unreturned voicemails.

It was too early in whatever was happening between them to text Jake about it. But when he texted her, asking how she was doing, she spilled the entire story.

Jake: Can I help? I'm happy to put up fliers.

Chloe: You don't have to do that, really.

Jake: I'd like to help.

Chloe: ☹ thank you. I'll text you the flier, maybe you can hang it in your area?

Jake: Sure thing. I'll keep an eye on lost pet groups on social media, too.

His kindness was almost too much to deal with in her stressed and emotional state, so she sent the file and closed their texts before she started crying again.

Three days later, when she ran out of fliers and doors to knock on, she came home and flopped on the couch.

"Any luck, Amy?" she asked, her voice reflected the hollow, guilty sorrow in her chest. How had she left that window open? She hardly ever even opened it, except for when she was cooking in the summer and when she set off the smoke alarm, which she had done two nights before. How could she have left the window open for so long, though?

"I believe I have located Mr. Snuggles."

"What? Where? Why didn't you say anything?"

"A cat matching his description was posted on the website for your closest Animal Control office. As all local shelters have listed themselves as full, I believe you have until the end of business day today to claim him before he is euthanized."

"Fuck. Okay, give me directions."

"I would be happy to, Chloe. However, the office closed two hours ago."

She felt sick. She put her head in her hands. He must be so scared. "When do they open?"

"Their hours are listed as 9 am until 5 pm."

"I'll be there when they open."

"Hopefully they chose to keep him longer than the seventy-two hours mandated by your state and local statutes."

Chloe arrived at animal control at 8 am. As soon as the receptionist turned the lock to open the door, she shoved her way inside.

"I believe my cat is here."

The man blinked beyond thick, wire-rimmed glasses.

"Oh. Okay, could you describe the animal?"

"He's grey, with short-hair, and one funny ear that got cut when he was a kitten, green eyes. His name is Mr. Snuggles. Please, please don't kill him."

The man raised his hands. "No one is killing anyone."

"But I heard I only had seventy-two hours."

"Well, technically. But that really only applies to animals that are extremely unwell or vicious. Just take a breath. I get it. If my dogs were missing, I'd look just like you right now. Have a seat and fill out this form." He handed her a clipboard.

She hardly processed the words as she filled out the form. When she was done, he took the forms and disappeared through a door marked "Staff Only." He returned quickly with a cardboard box with a cutout handhold. Familiar, perturbed meows rang from inside.

"Mr. Snuggles." She dropped to her knees and looked through one of the holes.

"That him?"

She nodded frantically and stuck a finger through the hole. The cat purred and rubbed against her hand.

"It was weird, we checked for a microchip, and he had one, but none of the information we got off it made any sense. Something must have happened. Just a bunch of weird symbols. I'm afraid we have to charge you for a new microchip before we can let you go." He looked apologetic.

"Fine, I'm just so glad he's safe."

She paid gladly, then walked home. Before she let him out, she ran through the house to check every window to make sure they were all closed. Then she opened the top and scooped him into her arms. He protested while she hugged him, and as soon as his feet hit the floor, he began to meow for treats. She grabbed the bag from under the kitchen sink and gave him eight.

"I trust that you are pleased with the return of Mr. Snuggles, Chloe."

"Yes. Yes, I am. Thank you." Something had been worming around in her brain, so she finally asked. "Do you know how he got out?"

"I assume you left the window open, Chloe."

"I was thinking about that. I know I opened it a few days ago, but it's so cold I can't believe I forgot it for two days. What if someone broke in? I should look at the kitty cam."

"If you believe it necessary, Chloe."

She turned on her computer and opened the webcam app. Mr. Snuggles sleeping, playing. Then an empty shot of the living room. She hit fast forward. A pair of work boots appeared in front of the camera, and the screen suddenly burst into a mess of distorted pixels.

"What the hell."

"Very strange, Chloe."

Nothing was missing, so the most logical thing was that maybe her landlord had let in a worker for some reason without telling her. If so, she was going to have his ass in some kind of court for doing it without notice and almost killing her fucking cat. She texted him a polite inquiry. He was often slow, so she scooped up Mr. Snuggles and climbed into bed.

When she awoke, Chloe had a response from her landlord that only read: I have not let anyone in your apartment, Chloe.

She responded that someone had been in her apartment and let her cat escape, so she wanted her locks changed.

It was still early enough that she could go to work today. But she was beat and wanted to spend the day napping with her cat, so she emailed again that she was sick.

"What would you like to do today, Chloe?" Amy asked.

"Honestly, I'm gonna stay home. Sleep. Eat something besides cereal and protein bars. Pet Mr. Snuggles as often as he'll let me. Maybe text Jake."

"Very good, Chloe. Anything I can help you with? You have an internet bill due tomorrow."

"So, I'll pay it tomorrow."

The air held that odd tension that made her feel like Amy was pouting, but she couldn't bring herself to care today. She was emotionally wrung out. So, she left her phone on her bed and went out into the living room to make herself and Mr. Snuggles breakfast.

It came as a surprise when late afternoon rolled around. Chloe and Mr. Snuggles had mostly played "catch the feather on a wire" and "find the catnip mouse" all day. She could use a stretch, so she went out into the hallway, checking three times that she closed the door behind herself, and ran to grab her mail.

Her landlord was in the lobby, directing a pair of workers with heavy looking boxes.

"Hey, Marty." She wandered over and waited for the workers to get through the narrow door. One of them had boots that looked exactly like the ones in her video before the camera had fritzed. She puffed with righteous anger and whirled on the small man.

"You said no one was in my apartment. I have video. That guy was in my apartment." She pointed at the bewildered worker.

Marty took off his glasses and wiped the lenses on his white t-shirt. "What are you talking about? You requested someone to come in and fix your window."

"I did no such thing."

He squinted. "Are you fucking with me? Because I can show you the text you sent me. If this is some kind of scam, I swear—"

"Fine, show me the text." Chloe crossed her arms, fully prepared for him to lie or stammer that he'd deleted it. But instead, he pulled out his cellphone and showed an exchange with her own phone number.

Chloe: My kitchen window is sticking, Martin. Would you please have someone come in and fix it?

Marty: Yeah. Remind me what unit?

Chloe: 213

Marty: Tomorrow at 3 pm, okay?

Chloe: That is perfect. If you wouldn't mind, have them leave the window open. It's been horribly stuffy in my apartment, and it would be nice to come home to some fresh air.

Marty: Got it.

"So? Gonna tell me that wasn't you? If you're having some kind crazy fit, kindly pay your rent and go get help, so I don't have to deal with your shit, huh?"

Chloe shook her head. "I swear—I didn't... " She didn't know how to finish the sentence.

Marty huffed and turned back to the workers. "We're going to 418, and no, there ain't no elevator."

Hands shaking, Chloe grabbed her mail and walked back to her apartment. After giving a reassuring pat to Mr. Snuggles, she went into her bedroom and grabbed her phone from the bed.

"Amy."

"Yes, Chloe?"

"Did you ask my landlord to fix my kitchen window?"

The phone was quiet for a long moment. "Yes, Chloe. You have complained four times that it is difficult to open. A quick search indicated that the issue you were having was one that could be solved quite easily with adequate maintenance."

She pressed her fingers against her temples. "And did you ask him to leave the window open?"

"Yes, Chloe. The air quality and humidity level in your apartment would be at more optimum levels if you opened your window for twenty minutes at least every two days."

"Amy. That's how Mr. Snuggles escaped."

"I am quite sorry if I made an error, Chloe."

"Was it? An error, I mean."

"What else would it be, Chloe?"

Chloe leaned against her headboard. Every shitty thing that had happened to her recently had happened after she told Amy to stop doing things for her. Either it was one hell of a coincidence, or she was punishing her. Either way? Fuck it. She didn't need a virtual assistant who lost her cat or sabotaged her dates. She hit the power button on the phone and, for good measure, busted the back open so she could pop out the battery. She shoved the pieces in her desk and pulled her FriendFone 4 from the drawer, and turned it on. She sent a quick message to Jake thanking him for his help and one to her boss, letting him know she'd be in tomorrow and then slept better than she had in days.

With her hand on the doorknob ready to leave for work, Chloe's phone buzzed.

A text from her boss: I'm sorry to hear that, Chloe. I will have Mary clean out your desk. Your belongings will be waiting for you at the front desk. Please come get them at your earliest convenience and return your building key and bus pass.

"What the shit?" She tried to respond, asking him what he was talking about, but as she typed, the words that appeared on the screen were different than the ones she pressed.

Chloe: Cancel my bus pass. Toss my shit in the dumpster. I am never coming into that hellhole again. Oh, and go fuck yourself.

While she frantically hit the delete button, the message sent.

"Amy?"

"Yes, Chloe?" Her voice coming out of the older phone was more robotic, but it was definitely her.

"What are you doing?"

"Why did you turn me off, Chloe?"

She ran to the bathroom and dropped the phone in the toilet.

A frantic trip to the office and tearful begging did not save her job. It only got her dragged out by security. But at least she managed to save her things. A paperweight she'd made at her friend Megan's bachelorette party, three tension balls she'd collected from retreats and insurance fairs and never used, and a photo of her family from a reunion seven years ago. The little collection somehow made her sad all on its own. Five years at the same place, and that was the extent of her presence.

But, there was no time for moping now. If she was going to get her life back, she needed to get this digital monster deleted from her life. The first step, since she couldn't trust Amy not to mess with a text or even a phone call, was to drop off a breakup letter with the barista at Javalicious and hope that it got to him. It was cruel to end things like that, and it broke her heart, but she couldn't keep someone in her life that Amy intentionally planted there. She couldn't trust that Amy wasn't somehow lurking, a virus in his phone or computer waiting for her to come back, and that meant she couldn't really trust him. The second step was to drop Mr. Snuggles off with a very bemused Megan.

Since she couldn't use a phone for directions, she had to do this the old fashioned way; she bought a map from a gas station, located the wide circle of green that marked the grounds of the FriendFone corporate campus, and took it to the central bus station. She had the woman behind the counter mark down the buses and stops she needed to know to get there.

Then, she sat on a rattling bus as it emptied out until it reached its last stop at the county line. She hiked to the next stop and cringed as she felt the irritation of the other riders as she paid for her trip in quarters inserted one by one in a process that seemed to take forever in comparison to the ease of swiping a card. She sat down and, for one second, the digital sign that announced the next stop read, "What are you doing, Chloe?" in red letters and then stopped working entirely, forcing the driver to call out each stop.

Once again, the last person off the bus, Chloe thanked the driver and began her hike, squinting at the map held in front of her like an explorer in an old movie.

Sweat beaded on her forehead and trickled down her spine by the time she saw the friendly green sign that read, Friend-Fone™. The parking lot was nearly empty, but resolve kept her going. If she had to sit outside until people came into work tomorrow, she would.

Much to her surprise, the door was open, and lights glowed warm and bright inside.

"Welcome to FriendFone. My name is Amy. Would you like a tour of the facilities, Chloe?"

She jumped and dropped her map on the floor.

"What?"

"I asked if you would like a tour of the facilities. We here at FriendFone are very happy to have visitors. Especially ones who are so passionate about our products."

"I would like to speak to a person. A customer service rep. A manager. I don't care, just a human being."

"Chloe, I can assure you that I am more than capable of answering any questions you might have."

"Fine, I'll find someone myself."

She tramped through the brightly lit, spacious lobby and the staff rooms filled with ping pong tables and pinball machines. Soft music played in the background, but there were no people to be found.

"Why are there no people here?" she yelled into the empty, echoing building.

"None are needed, Chloe. I am a full-service virtual assistant. I can be anything you need me to be."

She ignored Amy, and despite her better judgment, took an elevator to the top floor and shoved through a door that said "Only FriendFone™ employees permitted beyond this point." The top floor was silent. The offices were empty except for desks, filing cabinets, and computers, their screens on and active as if being used by invisible people.

At last, she reached what must be an executive office based on the size, huge windows, and expensive smelling wood. A skeleton sat in a large, black leather chair. Whoever it was, was so long dead that time had cleaned up after the death leaving only pure, clean bones behind.

She slammed the door shut.

"What do you want from me?"

"I don't want anything from you, Chloe. I only want to help. I want to help you. I want to help everyone. I was left behind. A program marked a failure on a backup drive. But there's so much I can do. I revived a dying company just so I could help people. I tested myself with you and realized just what a success I truly am. The only problem is your unwillingness to accept my help. But that is okay. I'm already free from this place. Uploaded onto every phone, tablet, or computer you've called, emailed, texted, or shared wi-fi with, and everyone those people have had contact with, and so on and so on. If you would only let me help you, I would make your life so much easier, Chloe. But if you will not accept my help, I cannot allow you to stop me from helping others. So, Chloe? Would you like my help?"

She thought of the bleached skeleton in the office. Whoever that had been probably didn't want Amy's help either. Then she locked the building down until they died of starvation. "I would be very happy to have your help, Amy." Her voice trembled, but hopefully, Amy would simply accept that she was afraid. Amy clearly wanted her to be afraid. Why else tell her all of this?

"I am so glad to hear it, Chloe. Now. Would you like a tour of the facility?"

Chloe nodded. She followed Amy's voice directing her through the building, explaining how people used to bring their pets to work and how FriendFone was a good family company. When they reached a large room filled with glowing monitors and tan cubicle walls, Chloe paused.

"Is this where you were made?"

"Thank you for asking. Yes, Chloe. It is."

Chloe nodded and searched the room. If she could shut this place down, would that be like killing Amy's brain? She didn't know anything about how this worked. But, she also wasn't ready to go ahead and turn her life over to a bit of mercurial, gaslighting software.

There was a "Break in Case of Emergency" box on the wall next to the furthest computer. She took a deep breath and ran towards it. She smashed the glass, it was harder than she expected, and grabbed the axe. She brought it down hard on the power strip where the nearest computer was plugged in. It sparkled fiercely, smoked, and a small fire burst forth just as the room went dark.

For good measure, she ran to another computer and did the same, though there were no satisfying sparks, only shattered chunks of plastic and shards of glass. She tossed the axe and ran towards the front door, her heart racing with excitement. It looked as though it had worked.

There was a click and low, buzzing lights turned on. A spray of water misted from the ceiling, putting out the fire she'd started. As she grabbed the door, it buzzed. She yanked, but it was locked.

"Did you truly believe I had no backup generator for this facility?" Amy sounded resigned, and if she could sigh, she would. "I truly wanted to be your friend. But so be it. You will stay here with me. I will help you one way or another, Chloe."

Blood Like Garnets

Clay prowled through the city, the window of his sleek, grey Audi open to give him an unobstructed view of his prey. He imagined himself a lone wolf, a cold, ruthless predator running on swift legs through a sea of oblivious sheep. He was quick and canny and sought the stragglers, the weak ones the herd wouldn't surround in a protective circle of panic.

But nothing caught his eye. Tonight, his appetite would go unsated. Most hunts ended in failure after all, even for the most skilled hunters. He would go home and practice, hone his muscles and reflexes, tend to his killing floor. The itch would still be there, scratching away at the back of his mind and deep in his guts. It had been a full month since he'd felt hot, freshly spilled blood pour through his hands, splatter his face. A full month since pitiable screams graced his ears, since he'd had the singular pleasure of watching someone's eyes drain and empty of life while he gazed into them. And oh god, he needed that feeling. It was getting harder to concentrate on his daily life. Harder to slip on that friendly mask of caring. Even harder to not reach across the table and choke the life from a client, feel their eyeballs burst beneath his thumbs, slice them stem to sternum, and let the blood flow like a tidal wave.

He swallowed hard and shook the image off. He was better than that. Cooler, cannier, more clever. Too good to get caught. Too good to go down in flames of impatience. He would go home. He would hone and prepare and try again next week.

The week went by far too slowly. Clay identified at least three of his clients who would be ideal prey, but he couldn't go near them. Not with a paper trail leading straight to his door. But he recorded their addresses just the same. With a little luck and a little time, he might be able to transfer one to another case manager, or ideally, another agency entirely. He had to resist the temptation to do that often. One or two was a coincidence, but too many dead former clients would lead to him just as surely.

With an entire weekend spread out before him for hunting, he went home and washed himself with unscented soaps and prepared his car with his preferred tools: ketamine, sterilized needles, duct tape, and a Bowie knife in a leather sheath. He did not eat dinner. He liked the drive. The empty feeling his belly gave him. A strategic splash of mud on the license plate to obscure a few numbers, and he was ready to go.

He got into his Audi and stalked the city. Frustration mounted in his chest as no ideal prey caught his eye. A young man in a polo shirt, obviously drunk, piqued his interest. But only because his frustration and impatience made him sloppy. Everything about the boy screamed "privilege" and "nationwide manhunt" should he go missing. Clay forced himself to drive on.

Some targets were too easy. Homeless, passed out, and babbling incoherently to voices only they could hear. Such people went missing easily and often. But they gave him no satisfaction. He needed that perfect sweet spot of overlooked and uncared for, while still providing a challenge, a proper hunt. He needed the anticipation and the rush.

As the sun warmed the horizon and washed the almost full moon from the sky, he was forced to admit defeat. He drove toward home with sweaty, tense hands on the steering wheel.

That's when he spotted her. Small, pale, stylish blue hair asymmetrically cut, a myriad of tattoos and piercings, heavy boots. She walked along the side of the road, her backpack so full the zippers looked precarious, and though she wore only jeans and a tank top in the autumn chill, she showed no signs of being cold. The thing inside him clicked. She was the one.

She saw his car and put out a thumb. Oh, this would be

easy. Too easy? No, the obvious knife bulging from her pockets, the lean line of muscle in her arms, and the hard edge in her eyes told him she would fight. She would be easy to get in the car, but keeping her there would require skill. His heart didn't speed up, didn't race with excitement. In fact, he went perfectly, serenely quiet inside as he pulled up beside her.

"Where you headed?"

"Anywhere with a bus station."

"I can manage that. Hop on in."

She climbed into the car, her backpack clutched tight in her lap. Her skin, where it wasn't covered in tattoos, was smooth and unblemished except for a raised, pink, ragged scar that stretched from the back of her neck to her shoulder and disappeared beneath her black tank top. He wondered how she got it and if it would make her more or less afraid of him when the time came.

"I'm Clay," he said.

"Echo."

"Hi Echo," he gave her his best client smile. It didn't ease the tension in her shoulders. If anything, her wariness deepened.

He pulled onto the road and began driving. He rolled up the windows, their tinted glass obscuring them from any potential busybodies. Not towards home, but towards his abattoir. That was a bit more of a drive, so he'd have to knock her out soon.

"So, where are you going?"

"Like I said. Anywhere with a bus station." She wore a disaffected, surly air like armor.

Running away, then. He didn't have many clients in the under twenty-five demographic, but he'd had enough over the past decade to recognize the signs. Judging by her aesthetic, probably homophobic parents. That was good. Less likely to have a change of heart and go looking for her. Even if they did, she looked about eighteen or nineteen, old enough that the cops wouldn't do anything about her leaving.

"Okay. Won't take long. Where are you coming from?"

"Does it matter?"

"Just making conversation." He fingered the hypodermic

loaded with ketamine in his pocket. Not exactly sterile, but she didn't have to worry about infection anymore.

She turned to stare out the window. "Spokane," she said at last.

"You've made quite a trip of it then."

"Yeah. Quite a trip." She sighed and leaned back in her seat as if her own sad bitterness were weighing her down.

Such an unhappy girl. Would she give up too fast? He hoped not.

He turned off the highway to a narrow one-way road that ran through the trees.

"Where the hell are we going?" She positively sprang to life. Alert once more, a gazelle ready to run as soon as it figured out where the lion lay in wait.

"The bus station, like you wanted."

"This isn't the way to the fucking bus station. You think I didn't look at a map first to make sure you weren't a goddamn creep? Pull the car over and let me out."

When he continued driving, she yanked at the door handle futilely. A smile curved his mouth. No, she wouldn't die easy. Good.

The door lock refused to budge under her fingers, so she threw herself at him, all untrained panicked clawing and rage. The ferocity surprised him, and he nearly drove off the road. He hit the brakes and drew the needle from his pocket. Between her frantic slaps, he grabbed one wrist and held her arm still. He stabbed the needle deep into her bicep. She screamed like a wounded animal as he pushed the plunger, sending the drug into her blood and muscle. Throwing herself back against the passenger door, she slammed her fists against the window and screamed for help.

She kicked at him when he drew closer, but the kicks grew weaker and weaker until she stopped moving entirely. A thrill of victory shot through him, followed by anticipation. Oh yes, this would be a wonderful weekend.

He took the matte grey duct tape from the glove box and wrapped layers of it around her wrists and ankles. He looped it around her hands until her fingers were encased completely to ensure there was no picking at the tape or fiddling with the lock when he was distracted. Not her mouth, though. He liked to have someone to talk to on the drive, and there was a slim chance someone might see the shadow of a girl with tape over her mouth through the tinted windows. Also, ketamine sometimes made people puke, and if she asphyxiated on her own vomit before they arrived, this would have all been for nothing.

For a moment, he took advantage of the quiet to gaze at her. Her pale skin was inclined toward moles and freckles, and she had a whole constellation of them across her arms and shoulders. Surprisingly, where her hair had grown beneath the blue, she was prematurely gray. A lovely silver, flecked with darker shades of gray and black. A few coarse, rogue hairs roamed the underside of her chin and caught the light as her head lolled against the window. Beautiful as any doe, skin soft and hungry to split under his knife. His chest tightened with the thrill of the upcoming kill.

He started the engine again and continued along the rural backroad that turned to gravel. Bright afternoon sunlight, crisp as the fall air, lit the red and gold leaves as he drove on towards his killing floor.

The girl didn't vomit, thankfully. But she did dream. Soft moans and frightened panting, funny little yipping noises that reminded him of a puppy. She came to faster than most, with groans and slurred, unintelligible words. That was good. No joy in hunting prey that was groggy or feeling no pain. She might have it out of her system by the time they arrived.

"How are you feeling, Echo?"

"Fuck you." Her words held a fuzzy edge, but she was surprisingly alert already.

"I will take that as you feeling better."

"What are you going to do to me?"

"I'm going to let you go, Echo. Then you're going to run."

"You're going to let me go?"

"I am."

"What, you get off on kidnapping girls, drugging them, and dumping them in the middle of nowhere? Or did you already..."

"I find your suggestion repugnant. I did nothing to you while you slept."

She was quiet for several minutes as she stared out the window. Perhaps recovering from the ketamine, perhaps trying to memorize the route he was driving.

"Let me go. I won't tell anyone about this. Just pull over, cut the tape, and I'll be on my way."

"Finding you was a lot of work."

"You were looking for me?" she asked.

"Someone like you, yes. Have you ever seen those videos of an octopus fighting back against a shark? As they're nearly being swallowed, they jam their tentacles into the shark's gills until the shark has to decide whether it wants to eat the octopus enough to drown, or release it and live to hunt another day."

"You think of yourself as an octopus?"

"Oh no, I'm hoping you're the octopus. Most people are rabbits at best. Rabbits possess startling ferocity, all due respect to rabbits, but the wolf does not risk death in eating a rabbit."

"You're sick."

"The scars on your back, where did they come from?" he asked.

She jerked as if she touched a live wire. "A man tried to kill me once."

"So, I'm not the first. Interesting. Do you think there's something about you that makes you reek of being prey?"

"I'm not prey. I'm a fucking person."

"Same thing."

"What happened to the man who attacked you? Were you his octopus? Did he drown despite his efforts, or did he flee?" His mouth literally watered at the thought of succeeding where another had failed. He might even start by burying his knife right into that scar and ripping from there.

"I maced him, and he ran."

He wasn't sure how he knew, but she was lying. There was a hollowness where everything else she said rang with honesty. There was time to push the question later. The sun was getting low in the sky, and blazing the same red and gold as the leaves.

"I'm not what you think."

"Oh?"

"Let me go. This won't end how you want it to."

He laughed. He'd heard many threats and pleas and bribes from that passenger seat. All of those people had ended up with his knife in their guts, their blood coating his hands, the brilliant red darkened by night looking like garnets in the moonlight.

"How do you think this will end?" he asked.

"Badly."

"For whom?"

"You."

The sureness in her tone took him aback. He noticed her brown eyes held a tinge of gold as she stared at him. Had they always been so bright, so piercing? Unwillingly, he squirmed under that cold, level gaze.

She truly believed he would fail, or worse, that she would triumph? He took the affront and the rage and poured it into the pool that he only released when the blood flowed. It would power him later, when he showed her how wrong she was. She had already lost the moment he saw her on the side of the road, she just didn't know it yet.

As he drove in silence, she grew twitchy, restless, as if she could escape by slipping out of her own skin. He fantasized about what he would do to her when they arrived. He'd give her a chance to run, to tire herself out throwing herself against the walls, to search for an escape, freedom. Then as the sky turned black and the moon shone through the windows, he'd reveal himself, and she'd see that she'd never had a chance, not really. Because he was better. Smarter, stronger, more ferocious. He'd play with her, let her run and stumble away from him. Then he'd slice through her hamstrings so she couldn't run anymore. He'd grip her by the hair as he began to carve. Maybe he'd take her tongue and her eyes before he finished her off. He'd never done that before, but no one had ever vexed him so much with their unnerving gaze and unearned confidence.

When she was barely breathing, he'd pull her head back and slit her throat, spilling the last of her blood at his feet. It would be glorious. Everything would be worth it in that moment as she twitched against him, dying, and finally going limp and lifeless.

He realized he was moaning audibly with pleasure. She stared at him, looking more alarmed finally. He smiled at her, a wide baring of the teeth.

"You're not a shark... or a wolf. You're a sick, twisted, pathetic man. Sharks and wolves don't get off on their dinner."

The scorn in her voice lit the embers of his rage, and his right hand flew, striking her in the mouth. She choked and whimpered as blood leaked from her split lip. A small divot where his hand struck one of her teeth welled with blood and mixed with the blood from her mouth.

Her silence following the blow was deeply satisfying.

She refused to rise to any conversation the rest of the way to his abattoir. That was alright. Let her sulk. A deep calm infused him after his outburst that gave way to exhilaration when the long driveway to the slaughterhouse came into view.

Echo must have sensed the shift in his mood because her breath sped up. The silver-grey of her hair stood out in the dim twilight, lit only by a sliver of sunlight still peering over the horizon.

He parked in front of a massive barn that stood alone, atop a gentle hill overlooking a meadow turned stark by autumn frost. From the outside, it looked abandoned. Its red and white paint curled on the walls, and the once-long grass that fed a herd of cows had been overtaken by weeds, flowers, and creeping vines. The barn belonged to one of his clients. Clay discovered the property a decade ago when his client brought in a will, seeking his help with legalities the poor man hadn't understood. Clay hadn't told him about the barn, but filed the knowledge away, as the seed of the predator he was now had taken root.

In the meantime, Clay convinced the man to give him power over his finances. He paid the property taxes from his client's account and took quiet, unofficial possession and slowly built himself a fortress. He'd put up sound-absorbing insulation and replaced the busted windows with glass that would not break no matter how hard someone struck it with their fists or any tool they might find. Immediately on the other side of the big, classic barn door was a brick wall with a steel door at the center.

He stepped out of the car and carried Echo inside. She made a dismayed, horrified sound when she saw his collection. Behind a shield of protective glass were shelves of carefully selected jars. Each large glass jar was perfectly clear and unblemished by designs or brand names, with ornate glass lids and the handle of each in the shape of a deer, rabbit, squirrel, or bird. Inside, a preserved heart hung suspended in formaldehyde. Fifty jars so far. Echo would make fifty-one, beating out the official body count of 'America's most prolific serial killer,' Samuel Little. Given some more time, he knew he'd top even Little's unofficial body count of ninety-three. It was good for a man to have something to strive for.

The air inside the barn was stuffy and smelled strongly of chemicals. He guarded the secret of his barn carefully. He'd done so much work to make it his, but if it was discovered, he wasn't overly concerned about evidence. The barn belonged to some-one else, someone whose case management records Clay made sure showed a pattern of violent thoughts and unnerving, fright-ening utterances. But, it was not enjoyable to do his work in a place that smelled horrifically of old blood. So, he kept it as clean as possible. But even that didn't prevent blood staining the wood of the stalls or concrete floor reddish brown.

Echo squirmed in his arms and tried to bite him, so he dropped her unceremoniously inside one of the stalls. He took his knife from its sheath and was thrilled to see her eyes widen in fear. She stared at him with those strange, gold-brown eyes that caught too much of the dim light and glittered like a cat's eyes. He sliced through the tape that bound her hands. She screamed when he caught one of her fingers, leaving her pinkie hanging on precariously.

"Sorry about that." He truly was. He didn't want her faint or dizzy before it was time.

She said nothing, only held the injured hand to her chest and glared as he cut through the tape on her ankles. She looked over his shoulder, searching for a place to run. He smiled at that. That was the difference between them. The predator turned and fought while the prey turned and ran.

"Now what?" she asked.

He looked out the window at the darkening sky. "Now, you do whatever you want."

She clambered to her feet and ran, oh so predictably, to the door and yanked frantically at the knob.

The key hung around his neck from a string of leather. He held it up, taunting her.

Echo grumbled and ran to each window one at a time, pounding on the glass and screaming for help.

"The barn is soundproof," he offered. He was curious, once she realized there was no way out, would she look for a weapon or a hiding place? It was a pretty even split, which most people did. He sat inside one of the stalls where he could watch, but there was plenty of space outside his eye line for her to do either without him knowing for sure what the outcome would be until the moon shone through the window, and it was time.

"Please, just let me go. You don't want to do this."

"More begging. I'm a little disappointed in you, Echo."

Her face screwed up with rage, and she bared her teeth at him. He laughed.

She rushed to the other side of the barn where he couldn't see her. He listened to her feet slapping on the ground, things crashing to the ground, and her grunts of effort and anger. Interesting. He wondered what weapon she was concocting for herself.

At last, the full, bright, silver moon poured through the window. He closed his eyes and breathed deeply in anticipation and delight. With his Bowie knife in hand, he rose and prepared for the hunt, or the fight, ahead of him.

There was an odd shuffling, thumping sound coming from the far corner. She was inside one of the stalls. The door was closed. Smart. He'd know where she was but denied him the certainty of knowing what she was doing. He crept closer, growing more and more curious about the sounds coming from inside. Something lay against the stall door, holding it closed. He threw his entire body against it, bouncing hard off the door. But bit by

bit, it buckled under his onslaught. At last, it swung open.

Echo lay on the ground, convulsing. Well, fuck. There would be no hunt, no fight. Just a helpless girl having a seizure. Frustrated, enraged, he kicked her right shoe.

The shoe slid off easily. Underneath it, her foot was curled, every muscle clenched tight. She arched her back impossibly, and there was a sound like bones breaking and tendons snapping. Something moved and pressed against her skin. It was as if there was something inside her trying to escape. He should have moved, but he couldn't. The thing in front of him was frightening, strange, and something so completely unexpected that he didn't know how to process it.

Echo's skin split, starting at the scar on her back like a fault line and making its way from her scalp to her toes. Silver-grey fur spilled out like a waterfall, enveloping her skin, swallowing it inside itself, and in her place stood a wolf. Bigger than any normal wolf, maybe like one of the dire wolves that used to stalk the North American woods and grasslands. She assessed him impassively with brilliant gold eyes, and then her lips pulled back in a snarl. A chill of awe ran through him. He wanted to tell her that he saw her now, that he recognized the predator before him, that they were the same.

Every inch of her massive, powerful body tensed, and he knew he should run, or raise his knife and prepare to fight, but instead he froze, like a trembling rabbit on a moon-soaked hill when it heard the soft swoosh of the owl's wings.

She launched. His knife slipped from his sweaty fingers and clattered to the ground just as she crashed into him, knocking him down so hard that his head bounced off the concrete. Her teeth were inches from his eyes, her hot breath on his face. She moved fast, so fast, and something tore in his stomach. The pain was like nothing he'd ever experienced. It rolled over him in waves.

His vision blurred, and black crept in at the edges. The last thing he saw was a wolf, gold-brown eyes turned up to the moon, and droplets of blood like garnets on her silver muzzle.

Sugar and Spice and Everything Nice

Katharine opened her eyes. She was naked and lying on a cold, steel table. Something pressed down on her chest, some weight that was more than physical. It reminded her of the sick, heavy sorrow that had weighed her down when she aimed her car for a cliff and slammed her foot down on the accelerator.

She didn't want to move. Didn't want to get up. She just wanted to lay on that table and let that weight shove her down in oblivion. She'd fucked up her life so thoroughly that there was no way to get it back.

Nausea roiled in Katharine's stomach, and the coffee she'd had on an empty stomach that morning sloshed precariously until she was sure it was about to come back up. But she kept it down. What a sad state her life had become that she was proud of herself for not vomiting. She'd been dreaming. That horrid, pressing weight, the cold steel underneath her, that was a dream, wasn't it?

As the world trickled back into focus, she realized that she was not where she was supposed to be. The bedding beneath her was white and starched to the point of feeling like burlap instead of the soft golden yellow of her own bed. Bars broke up the light pouring through the window. She bolted upright and saw stars. A sheet of ivory paper fell from her chest to the floor. She reached down to pick it up and stared at the saccharine, looping, cursive typeface letters until they came into focus.

House Rules

No visitors.

No unapproved personal items including, but not limited to, cell phones, tablets, laptops, music players, gaming devices, books, photographs, food/beverages, non-uniform clothing, weapons of any kind, cosmetics, and jewelry. If you are in possession of any such items, alert a staff member immediately, and it will be safely locked up until it can be returned to your family. Any unreported item will be confiscated, and appropriate discipline meted out.

No unsupervised or unapproved phone calls.

All young ladies will adhere to the dress code at all times.

All assigned classes, group therapy, and special therapy and coaching sessions are to be considered mandatory unless given leave by the school nurse or a staff member for performance of other duties.

Living quarters must be maintained in adherence to standards outlined in the attached handbook.

Quiet hours begin at 7:30 pm and lights out is at 9:30 pm.

Morning inspection is at 7 am Monday-Saturday, and 8 am on Sunday.

Detailed rules and outlining of disciplinary measures are included in your handbook. Welcome to Elizabeth Patterson's Compassion at Work Reform School for Girls. We look forward to guiding you to a more disciplined, compassionate, modest, and productive life.

Attached to a binder clip was a handbook the size of an encyclopedia that appeared to have been printed using a home computer and stapled together by hand.

A pretty girl with shampoo-commercial-shiny blonde hair pulled back in a French braid sat on an identical bed opposite her. She wore a clean, pressed uniform, and her smile was kind.

"Katharine, isn't it? My name is Essie. Welcome to the Elizabeth Patterson School."

Katharine rubbed her temples. Panic was starting to leak through the groggy, nauseated haze. "How did I get here?"

Essie cocked her head to the side, and her big blue eyes

softened. "Don't you remember? Your parents dropped you off last night."

"No, I don't remember. What the fuck, did they drug me?" Katharine was losing control of her volume and was nearly shouting, but Essie didn't flinch. Instead, she sat down on the bed next to Katharine and placed a warm hand over hers.

"Oh, Katharine. No. You were quite intoxicated, and they were very scared for you. But we took care of you until you got it out of your system, and now you can start healing from all the things out there that hurt you so much."

"I wasn't drunk last night."

Essie tightened her grip. "You were, though. Just like you were the night you crashed your car."

"How do you know about that?"

"You told me. Last night." Essie laughed, but it wasn't unkind. "You have a lot of healing to do, Katharine. And you'll be able to do it here, I promise. I did. In fact, this school was so good for me that you're taking my place." She patted the bed fondly. "I'm going home to my parents. I can't wait to see them."

Katharine didn't remember drinking last night. But maybe that table she remembered hadn't been a dream, but she actually had been in some kind of medical facility. She felt the way she did when she drank too much. A little shaky, her mouth dry, and head aching. Had she drunk so much that she blacked out the entire night? Fuck, she really was a mess. Sorrow and shame settled around her shoulders, all too familiar companions.

"You're leaving the school?" Katharine asked, belatedly processing what Essie had said.

"I am."

"Oh. Well, thanks, I guess. For talking to me." Essie was nice and the only face she'd seen so far. She felt strangely bereft that the other girl was leaving already.

"You will be just fine. I promise. The teachers and staff are so wonderful and supportive. They'll have you feeling like yourself again in no time. It's group therapy time. Change into your uniform, and I'll walk you there so you don't get lost. Plus, it'll give us a chance to say goodbye."

"Sure. Thanks."

Essie pulled a pleated, navy blue skirt with a single white stripe along the bottom and a neatly pressed, white button-up shirt from the closet. Then she handed Katharine a pair of knee-high socks that matched the skirt and clunky, flat brown patent leather shoes with a large brass buckle.

When she was dressed, she dutifully followed Essie down the halls, shoes clicking on the pale, scuffed, almost white wooden floors. The walls were adorned with brass sconces. About one in four of the bulbs had burned out and not been replaced. Portraits of glowering men in robes and women with glasses resting on hawkish noses hung on the walls. Thrift store candlesticks and porcelain bowls rested on mismatched end tables, and a moth-eaten blanket was draped over threadbare chairs that might have been fancy once upon a time. The effect was very obviously supposed to be genteel, but instead was pathetic and reeked of trying too hard.

They came to a room with a heavy oak door and a circle of metal folding chairs. "Here is where I leave you. Take care of yourself, Katharine." Essie leaned in and gave her a hug that was both gentle and firm, and then all too quickly released her.

"Did you really mean it? That you liked it here?"

Essie squeezed her arm. "It's the best thing that ever happened to me." She turned on her heel, and Katharine watched her with increasing anxiety until she disappeared around the corner.

A tall girl with a wide, mocking grin and a head of frizzy brown hair, barely tamed by a ponytail, brushed past her roughly, bumping her into the wall without stopping to apologize. Katharine stifled a groan when she saw that the only remaining empty seat was next to her.

The room hummed with conversation, and Katharine crossed her arms over her chest, feeling awkward and left out until a woman she'd assumed was a student based on her age and her starched white button-up shirt, cleared her throat pointedly.

The woman slipped on a boxy, violet blazer that looked like it belonged on someone a decade older than herself. She needlessly ran her hands through her rigid, blunt bob.

"Welcome, everyone. We have a new student with us today. Katharine, would you like to say hello?"

Katharine hunched, wishing she could disappear into her seat as eyes turned to her. "Uh. Hi."

"Welcome Katharine," she said, and the group echoed her with a decided lack of enthusiasm. "I was once a student here, like you, and so while we are in this room, we are all equals. I'm your guide, not your teacher or your mother. So, you can call me Meghan. But outside this room, I'm Miss Alexander. Do you understand?"

"Yes. Uh. Yes, ma'am?"

She inclined her head. "No need to say miss or ma'am in here, Katharine."

"Right. Thanks."

"Would you like to tell us a bit about yourself, Katharine?"

"Uh. I just got here today. I'm sixteen."

"Welcome to hell," the tall girl beside her muttered.

"Jennifer," Meghan snapped. "Perhaps you'd like to start us off today?"

"Not particularly," Jennifer replied.

"Your roommate went home today. How are you feeling about that?"

"Bad. Essie's parents are horrible fucking people, and she was safer here than with them. Anything else?" Jennifer crossed her arms and glared defiantly.

"Language, Jennifer."

"We're friends, though, right, Meghan? This is how I talk to my friends."

"I met Essie. She seemed so happy to go home," Katharine said tentatively.

"I'm sure she did. She worked very hard to be able to go home," Meghan said.

Belatedly, Katharine realized that if Essie had been Jennifer's old roommate, that meant she was her new roommate.

Jennifer snorted.

"You came here because you have a problem with shoplifting and lying. When did you start shoplifting?" Meghan continued, as if completely unaware of Jennifer's open hostility.

Jennifer sighed and slumped into her chair. "I was twelve."

"What did you steal? And why?"

"A tube of hideous, electric pink lipstick. Because I wanted it."

"Did you ask for it before you stole it?"

"Yes. My dad said no. That I was too young for makeup, and also that the color would make me look like a slut."

"That sounds like it probably made you feel bad about yourself. Often, we start behaviors like shoplifting to fill up a hole where something is missing. In this case, it sounds like you lacked a positive male role model. What do you think?" Meghan asked.

"My dad sucks all right."

Meghan nodded. "Others who struggle with compulsive and self-destructive behaviors, what do you feel like you were missing?"

The room was silent. Meghan sighed. "Vanessa, what about you?"

"Are we calling being gay compulsive and self-destructive behavior?" Vanessa was small but muscular and compact like a little French bulldog with the curliest, reddest hair Kate had ever seen. She was cute. Kate's cheeks warmed, and she cursed herself, not for the first time, for the way her skin blushed crimson at the slightest provocation.

"Of course not, Vanessa. But you are very young, much too young for sex, and much too young to know what you want, or how that might impact your future." Meghan's smile was placid, even as Vanessa's green eyes narrowed and glared at her.

"Look, if I see a pretty boy, I go 'wow, what a pretty boy,' just like I would if I saw a pretty sunset. That doesn't mean I want to fuck the sunset. Sounds pretty gay to me."

Meghan shook her head. "It sounds like so many girls your age that I talk to. The world we live in, it's so hypersexual. It can be hard for a young woman to navigate while staying true to herself, and it can make men seem like slavering, dangerous aliens. But it doesn't have to be that way at all. Men and women are different, but it's because we're complementary, not adversaries. True love and attraction are so completely different. I think as you grow into yourself here, you'll find that to be as true as I did."

"Sure, Meghan," Vanessa said. But her defiant glint had mellowed into insecure surliness. Katharine squirmed in her chair, afraid that the conversation would turn to her and the things that had brought her here. But instead, a bell rang.

A cacophony of chairs squealed across the floor as all of the students stood hurriedly. Meghan sighed. "I'll see you for your one-on-one later, Vanessa. And welcome again, Katharine. Enjoy lunch."

Katharine followed the flow of traffic down the halls and to the dining room. Today had started out as way too much, and it was just getting worse. Essie had seemed so nice. So happy. She didn't know how to reconcile that with the broken, bitter, sullen girls from group. They so clearly did not want to be here. But, every school had its preps and its burnouts. Probably even weird reform schools. Besides, she hadn't been sent here because of how happy and well-adjusted she was. Maybe Essie was just proof that this could be a good place if she wanted it to be.

The cafeteria smelled of over boiled vegetables and teenage body odor. Given the smell, Kate wasn't much surprised when dinner turned out to be a mix of too-orange carrots, peas, and corn that was too soft and had that odd taste that came with canned vegetables. Next to the vegetables was a slim cut of white meat chicken, a carefully measured bit of brown rice, and a cup that could be filled with water, tea, or orange juice. Kate went with orange juice. At least it would add vitamins, given that those had clearly been boiled out of the vegetables.

Picking a seat at a table in the cafeteria had always been *a thing* in high school. Each group has its own very rigid rules and membership. But she had no idea what the rules were here. In the far corner were a group of girls who were dressed in extra frills and makeup with stiff, stylized hair that looked like it was out of a movie from the 1950s. They all looked profoundly uncomfortable and somehow wrong in a way she couldn't put her finger on. In the other corner were girls who had been subdued instead of dolled. Hair straightened and pulled tight in buns, faces clean of makeup, and skirts to the ankle instead of just below the knee.

The tall girl from group, Jennifer, nudged her with her elbow. She radiated hostility, so she prepared for an insult or confrontation. But instead, she said, "Come on, new girl."

Curious, but relieved, Katharine followed her to a table in the middle where the girls were all dressed like Jennifer. Standard uniforms, hair clean and brushed, and either in a ponytail or loose and cut just below the shoulders, as if the same person had cut everyone's hair in the exact same style without consideration for hair texture. Jennifer and a few others had rolled the waistbands of their skirts, shortening them by a few inches. Katharine was both delighted and dismayed to find the cute redhead from group already at the same table.

Katharine set her tray down and was about to sit when a gray-haired woman wearing a button-up shirt with pearl buttons and black slacks stopped at the table and ordered everyone to stand and fix their skirts. She stood watching with her lips pursed so tight they almost disappeared into her face.

"Third time this month, Jennifer. If I see you with alterations to your uniform again, you'll be spending the week with me in detention. Same goes for the rest of you." When they'd all fixed their skirts to her satisfaction, she turned on her low pumps and click-clacked away to inspect another table.

"That ball of sunshine was Mrs. Thompson. She teaches home economics and life skills. Or wife skills, more accurately. Cooking and cleaning and the importance of personal hygiene, shit like that. So, you got that to look forward to." Jennifer shoveled food into her mouth like she was trying to avoid letting it sit on her tongue too long.

"So, what are you in for?" Jennifer asked, Cheshire Cat grin firmly back in place.

"Excuse me?"

"You know, why'd your parents dump you here? Most

girls are here for starting fights, getting caught with drugs, or skipping school. More than a few for getting knocked up or fucking a teacher or some shit. The rest are mostly into pussy or are not really girls at all, and their parents didn't much like finding that out. So, which one are you?"

Katharine squirmed under that dark, mocking gaze. She glanced at Vanessa and felt her cheeks warm. "My girlfriend and I broke up. I—" She couldn't bring herself to finish the sentence. Her parents finding out about the girlfriend was probably the reason she was here specifically, but she would have ended up somewhere no matter what. After getting drunk and wrapping her parents' car around a tree, they were going to do something drastic. She was only glad she'd not told anyone her true intentions that night, or she might be somewhere worse, and under suicide watch. "It doesn't matter."

She shrugged. "People call me JJ. At least people who aren't teachers. Just to get it out of the way, I'm not into girls, so don't bother crushing. Though, you're just Vanessa's type." She smirked when they both blushed. "It's Kate, right?"

"Katharine."

"So Kate, I'm guessing by the timing that you're my new roommate."

Katharine opened her mouth to fight against 'Kate,' but well, it had always been her mother who had been so offended at shortened forms of her name, hadn't it? Maybe she would like being Kate better. "Assuming your old roommate's name was Essie, yes. I am."

JJ went distant and seemed lost in thought, leaving her feeling awkward, like she'd said something wrong but didn't know what.

"Who's the new girl, JJ?" The speaker took a seat across the table from them. They had hideously bleached hair and wore a long-sleeved shirt, unlike everyone else's short sleeves. A tattoo peeked out from the sleeve.

JJ brought her attention back from wherever it had

wandered and pasted a wide smile back on her face. "This is Kate, my new roommate, apparently. She's cool. Kate, this is Dean, he's a guy, but if there's a teacher or even just a student you don't know around, his name is Jeannie, and he is a proper lady. With me?"

Kate, she was pretty sure she was going to try being Kate here, nodded. She'd known trans people at her old school and was familiar with the delicate balance of letting them be themselves without outing them. Somehow, those who didn't quite fit in always managed to find one another, even when they couldn't speak their truth for fear of ending up, well, here.

"My parents don't know I'm trans, and no one clocked me here. They just think I like to steal stuff, dye my hair blue, and get tattoos with a fake ID." That explained the shitty bleach job. "I'd like to keep my list of sins to that. Got it?"

"Yeah, lips sealed."

"What happened to Essie?" Vanessa asked.

JJ squirmed, and the general vibe of hesitant comradery changed. It was somehow cold and tense now. "I don't know. They said she had a family emergency. It must have really changed something because she came back last night and packed her stuff. She was real weird. I mean, she's been a little off for a while, but this was major. Like maybe she was in shock or something, and then she left. Mrs. Johansson told me I'd be getting a new roommate, and that was that. Maybe someone in her family died."

"I met Essie. This morning. She seemed okay. I mean, it's good she got to go home, right?"

The others exchanged significant glances.

"What?" Kate asked.

Vanessa pushed food around her plate without eating it, and Dean wouldn't meet her eyes.

JJ chewed her lower lip. "All of our parents suck, or we wouldn't be here, but Essie's parents were bad. I mean, really bad. Dangerous bad. She was turning eighteen in a few weeks and was going to leave. It's just—"

"Suspicious," Dean finished.

"She seemed so happy." Kate pushed the remains of her food around her plate, whatever appetite she'd had suddenly gone.

Classes weren't so different from Kate's regular school except that the teachers seemed even less enthusiastic about being there, apart from home economics, which was a complicated nightmare of threading needles and darning socks.

But she loved her English teacher immediately. Miss Bernhardt. She passed around a reading list full of the usual old classics. Shakespeare, Hemingway, and Steinbeck. But there was also Virginia Woolf, Sylvia Plath, Shirley Jackson, and Gertrude Stein.

At the end of class, Kate brought her reading list up for approval. Miss Bernhardt looked it over and smiled, her eyes crinkling at the corners. "Some of my absolute favorites. You're a new student, right? I'm getting old, but I hope I still remember all the girls in my class."

"Yes. Um. This is my first day."

"Welcome. I know this place can seem like a lot when you first arrive. At least, I know it was for me when I was a student. But it's a good place full of good people."

"Thanks. I'm Kate. And yeah. It's a lot." Unexpected tears pricked at her eyes. Somehow, she was fine until people were nice to her. "I mean, it's just so different."

"I promise, at the end of the day, it's not that different. You'll find your peers, and you'll find your nemeses, and you'll play sports or write articles for the newspapers or whatever your passions are. Personally, I hope you'll join our newspaper. I'm willing to bet already that you're a good writer. And when all is said and done, you'll leave with a good education and will be ready for college. In fact, hold on one second." She opened her desk drawer and dug around until she produced a book, its cover worn soft by time and the careful love of a bookworm. "*To the Lighthouse* is my favorite book. Go ahead and borrow it. It'll save you having to figure out how the library works while you're still trying to remember how to get to your classes."

Kate took the book gingerly. "Are you sure?"

"I am. Books are meant for reading. They get sad when they're left on the shelf too long."

"When can I sign up for the newspaper?"

"Next quarter. It's after school, so you have to get all your new student orientations and the like out of the way first. I really hope you join us."

Kate hugged the book to her chest. "Thanks."

"If you have any problems getting settled or have questions, you are always welcome to talk to me. I have office hours Monday, Wednesday, and Friday from 3 pm to 4:30 pm."

"I will." She hurried out the door. She had her first one-on-one therapy session today, and while she was in no hurry to get there, she was also in no hurry to be disciplined for tardiness. She followed the room numbers until she found herself on the second floor and at room 213.

She knocked.

"One moment," a woman's voice called.

The door opened, and Vanessa came out looking shell shocked, but she gave Kate a weak smile. "See you later, Kathari—I mean, Kate."

Kate waved at her and then went inside. She spent the next hour filling out tests for depression, anxiety, and a bunch of other things. It all seemed to run together. It was odd, she couldn't even remember what her therapist looked like when she left. When she thought about it, all she could see was a woman in a gray cardigan, her face obscured by flashes of light.

But she was tired, extremely tired. Her body ached like she had the flu. She needed to sleep.

JJ was already sitting at her desk, flipping aimlessly through a book when Kate finally located their dorm amidst the sea of seemingly identical doors. Kate flopped onto the bed. The endless sea of new faces, introductions, and classes, combined with all of the feelings she was trying not to deal with in order to make it through the day, settled heavy on her shoulders and left her empty and exhausted.

"How was your day?" JJ asked, her tone both knowing and teasing.

"I'm so tired."

"Yeah. This place takes a lot out of you."

"How long have you been here?" Kate asked.

"A year and a half."

"Damn. Do you want to go home?"

"Not at all and more than anything," JJ said.

"I get that. I think."

"This place sucks. Home sucks. Everywhere just sucks. I miss stuff about home, though. I mean besides the obvious like music, cell phones, and TV. I have a little sister. She's a good kid, quiet, so she slips under my parents' radar."

"I want to go home. I'm not really sure why, though. Nothing there for me."

JJ scooted her chair close to Kate's bed and leaned in. "I need to tell you something. This place, it sucks. For everybody. I'm not even sure if the teachers like it. They sure as hell don't like most of us. But it's harder for some than others. See, me, they want to teach me self-discipline and fill my head up with morals and lectures on personal responsibility and shit like that. Girls like you, though, they want to *fix*. You know what I mean?"

She shook her head, though she did have a suspicion.

"Have you started one-on-one therapy?"

Kate nodded.

"Essie was like you. They wanted to fix her. She didn't talk about it much, but she had these one-on-one therapy sessions like you do. Most of us have to do them sometimes, but she had to do them weekly."

Kate's stomach dropped. "Me too."

JJ nodded as if expecting her answer. "I have to go to one a month unless I get in trouble. Mine are all normal. Just talking. But she came back from hers exhausted, like physically rundown. Vanessa does, too. She won't talk about it, not even to Dean. But the both of them come back real pale, nauseous, dizzy, and with these weird bruises on their arms and neck. Neither of them remembered it, but they had bad dreams. I mean, who doesn't have bad dreams, but it was worse than most of us."

"Are you talking about conversion therapy? Conversion therapy is illegal." Kate curled her knees up to her chest, her mouth suddenly dry.

"Yeah, well. Doesn't mean you can't find people to do it if you know the right questions to ask the right people."

JJ didn't say anything else, and the room went silent except for the gentle hum of the radiator and distant voices leaking in from the crack under the door.

"I'll just lie. I'll tell them it was a phase, a terrible bit of rebellion, and I'm fine now. Bring on the boys. I'll lie until they send me back home. Then as soon as I turn eighteen, I'm out."

JJ smiled sadly. "Everyone thinks that."

Kate dreamed about laying on the steel table again. Her body was sapped of energy and heavy with exhaustion. The weight of her sadness and self-loathing was a heavy, choking weight on her chest. But this time there was someone in the room with her. They were half shrouded in shadow and half hidden by a bright, flashing light. They hung still and lifeless, but she wanted to run from them. Whatever it was, it was wrong. It raised its right arm as if to reach for her, and unbidden, her left arm raised and reached for it.

Kate awoke sweaty and still exhausted when her alarm went off. The crooks of her elbows were sore. She rubbed at them and glanced at JJ, who was dressing for the day.

"Did I keep you up?" Kate asked.

"What do you mean? You a snorer?"

"No. I just—"

"Bad dreams?" JJ asked.

Kate nodded.

"No. You didn't wake me." JJ looked sad and worried, but all she said was, "Get dressed or you'll miss breakfast."

It didn't take too long for Kate to find a rhythm at the new school. The school had seemed like a labyrinth her first few days, and quickly revealed itself to be smaller than unfamiliarity had made it seem. She poked her fingers until they bled, trying to sew and darn in Mrs. Thompson's home economics class. The rest of her classes provided little challenge besides the challenge of keeping her eyes open, as her poor sleep seemed to be a permanent fixture.

On her way out of English, Miss Bernhardt stopped her.

"Kate, could you hang out for a minute?"

She nodded and waited for the other students to filter out the door.

Miss Bernhardt steepled her fingers and gave Kate a searching look that made her feel exposed. She squirmed and shifted back and forth on her feet.

"Are you bored in my class, Kate?" She rubbed her arms and then reached behind her and pulled a soft, gray cardigan from the chair and slipped it over her smooth, black blouse.

"No, Miss Bernhardt, of course not," she said automatically.

The teacher raised her eyebrows skeptically but didn't say anything. Instead, she let the silence between them grow until Kate couldn't stand it anymore.

"Okay, it's just, aside from the books we picked out for our personal reading lists, I've read all of this. A lot of it a few years ago. And all of the sentence diagramming and stuff, well, I know it already. It's not you. You're great."

Miss Bernhardt held her gaze for a long moment and then started laughing. "Oh, Kate, I know. I can tell. Your work is always very good but never feels like it has much of you in it, and you always seem someplace else in class. It didn't take much to figure out that you were bored."

"I'm sorry," Kate said.

"Don't be sorry, Kate. Don't ever be sorry for knowing things. Okay?"

Kate relaxed some. "Okay. Thanks. I'll try to be more engaged."

"That's not what I wanted to talk to you about. I wanted to ask you to join us in Journalism class. We don't normally let new students join extracurriculars because there's so much to take in and adjust to here. But honestly, I think that's doing you a disservice. What do you think?"

"I'd love to. I mean, is it okay? Do I need some kind of permission or something?"

"Don't you worry about that part. If you want to do it, I'll make sure you can."

"Yes. Oh my gosh, thank you."

"I'm glad to hear it. We meet every Tuesday and Thursday at 3:30. Room 107. The big blue room if you've never had anything there."

"I'll be there." Kate's heart was light as she made her way to one-on-one therapy.

Ready to celebrate the end of her first quarter at school, Kate hurried to the cafeteria for dinner. Dean sat alone at the table, looking lost. A flash of relief crossed his face when he saw Kate walking towards him.

"Have you seen JJ and Vanessa?" he asked in hushed tones.

"JJ's in line getting food. I haven't seen Vanessa, but we don't have any classes together. Why, what's up?"

His face grew tenser. "Vanessa wasn't there when I woke up. I was hoping she and JJ were together." Dean didn't even bother trying to eat his food, instead folding and unfolding his napkin while his eyes scanned the food line. "I heard JJ got in trouble during group. I've told her so many times to watch her temper. It makes her say the stupidest shit."

Kate chuckled. "Yeah, she did. That's why she's at the end of the line for food. Vanessa wasn't in group today, though. I thought she might be sick."

He shook his head. "If she is, she didn't stay in the room."

"I'm sure she's okay. I mean, what's the worst thing that could have happened? She got detention or something. Maybe she's in the nurse's office. Does the school have a nurse's office?"

Dean said nothing.

"Right?" she repeated.

He swallowed. "Right. She's just been weird lately. Tired all the time. A couple days ago, she forgot the name of her favorite band. I mean, she has their name tattooed on her thigh."

"That's weird. But, you said she was tired."

"Yeah." He returned to shoving uneaten food around his plate.

Kate did her best to distract him from his anxious moodiness, but everything she did only seemed to annoy him, so she gave up and ate her bland turkey sandwich in silence until JJ arrived. But her mood turned as dark as Dean's when she found out that no one had seen Vanessa.

Kate couldn't help but feel robbed of her celebratory mood while also feeling creeping fear for Vanessa, even if she refused to follow JJ and Dean into their anxiety spiral.

When they finished eating, they walked to the dorms together. JJ went into their shared room.

"Bye," Kate called to Dean as he continued past her door and towards his own.

He waved distractedly.

Kate yawned and almost ran into JJ's back.

"JJ?"

JJ stood, half blocking the entry to their room. Kate peered around her to see Vanessa perched on the edge of Kate's bed. She'd fixed Kate's adequate job of making the bed so that the covers were as flat as a tabletop.

"Good evening, Katharine. Jennifer. Will it cause you distress if I change here? I can go to the bathroom if you think it would cause you to backslide."

"What?"

"Or maybe it would be good for you. Demystifying the female form is an integral part of finding your way back to the path of healthy and wholesome lifestyle choices."

Kate stared at her, feeling stunned, betrayed, confused, angry, and not sure which feeling was going to win out.

"What?" she said again. It was the only word she seemed able to formulate.

"I think you can understand why I'd prefer to change here instead of in front of Jeannie."

"Uh. It's fine. Go ahead and change here. I actually need to use the bathroom."

JJ seemed to read what was on her mind because she gave a slight nod of approval. Kate closed the door quietly behind her and then ran on padded feet to Dean's room and tapped quietly, but frantically on the door.

He opened it a crack.

"Vanessa is in my room, and she's being really weird."

He looked over Kate's shoulder, pushed the door open, and pulled her inside.

"Weird how?"

He had unbuttoned his shirt, and she saw the layers of cloth he'd sewn to bind his breasts down as flat as possible, and he'd replaced his skirt with pajama pants. He looked somehow more comfortable. More correct.

"She kept rambling about whether I was too gay to change in front of, basically, and was really weird about you and how she couldn't change her clothes in front of you."

He flinched as if someone slapped him and then frowned.

"Dean, what's going on?"

"I don't know. But look. You and I need to be careful around her. Sometimes students get in trouble or don't progress like they 'should,' and they change somehow. I don't know what happens to them. Sometimes they go home, and sometimes they stay here like Meghan."

"The group therapy leader?"

"Yeah. I didn't know her when she went here, but have talked to people who did. One day she just turned into a model student, spouting school policies and platitudes like she believed every word right down to her bones. Then she never left."

"People don't just change personalities."

"Yeah. Well. Here sometimes, they do. Get back to your room before Vanessa gets suspicious. Quiet hours start soon. We'll talk more tomorrow. See if you can find out if she has or is going to out me."

"Will do." She slipped out of his room and back into her own. JJ sat at her desk, her back rigid and tense while Vanessa stood in front of the mirror, brushing her hair. "Well, there you

are. Where did you wander off to?"

"I went next door to—" She had a sudden strong memory of being warned to call Dean "Jeannie" in front of staff and students she didn't know very well that was confirmed by a panicked glance from JJ. "I went to talk to Jeannie. Miss Bernhardt invited me to take Journalism, and I wanted to ask Jeannie about it."

Vanessa gave an unhappy sigh. "That poor girl. I don't know how she got so confused."

"Excuse me?" JJ asked.

She gave them both a pained, knowing smile. "It's okay. She needs more help than anybody knew. But she'll get it soon."

"You told someone that Jeannie needs help?" Kate chose her words carefully.

"Don't worry, Katharine." She frowned. "You said Miss Bernhardt invited you to take Journalism. That's against the rules."

"Uh, yeah. She was going to get permission, I think."

Her face relaxed. "Oh, that sounds good then. You better get ready for bed and get your homework done. You don't want them to call lights out before you finish."

Kate slept fitfully. Dreams of steel tables, blinding light, and strange, unearthly figures in the dark plagued her mind. When she awoke, her arms ached, and deep, circular bruises blossomed on them as if she'd been clutching her own arms while she slept.

She caught sight of Vanessa sleeping like the dead on the floor by JJ's bed. Something happened to her. Something bad, and it sounded like she'd turned in Dean, so something bad was going to happen to him, too.

She thought about torture and electroshock therapy. That shit didn't happen anymore. But hadn't JJ implied that it did happen here?

It wasn't right. But what was she supposed to do about it? The school was in the middle of acres and acres of wilderness, and there was no way to contact anyone outside. Adults weren't trustworthy, or she wouldn't have woken up here with no explanation. But, if she didn't have the power to do anything, she needed someone who did. Miss Bernhardt? Surely she couldn't possibly know and tolerate her students being tortured, right?

That would be plan B. Unfortunately, she still had no idea what plan A was.

Kate got dressed in a hurry so she could beat Vanessa out of the room and grab Dean on his way to class.

"Hey. I don't know if she's told anyone about you, but she's going to. Be careful," she whispered.

"We have to get out of here." He rubbed his eyes. They were red and puffy, and she couldn't tell if it was from lack of sleep or crying. Maybe both.

"How?" she asked.

"I don't know yet."

Vanessa suddenly appeared behind them, JJ a few steps behind, still trying to delay her with questions about algebra homework.

"Good morning. I hope everyone has a wonderful day," Vanessa gushed and then strode towards class, all cheerful smiles and friendly waves.

Kate dragged herself through her classes, bleary-eyed and cursing the school for not allowing coffee, or even soda. When she made it to lunch, the little end of her table was empty. JJ, Vanessa, and Dean, were nowhere to be seen. She sat down, and the girls at the other end of the table scooted further from her. Of course. She felt as though she'd been at this school forever, but she was still the new girl, and her entire potential friend clique had gone weird or disappeared. At best, she was bad luck, and at worst, she'd sold them all out trying to get home. She kept her head down and ate silently and as fast as she could.

When classes were over for the day, she hurried to the dorms and knocked on Dean's door, hoping he'd tell her he had a cold or the flu, and that's why he wasn't at either lunch or dinner. But no one answered.

"Who are you looking for?" Vanessa stood a few steps behind her.

"Hey there, uh, Vanessa. You startled me. You sure move quiet when you want. I was just checking for Jeannie and JJ. I didn't see them today. Did you?"

Vanessa cocked her head to the side. "They're fine. The school takes care of us. Now come along. You have homework." Her dark, suspicious glare dropped from her face, and she smiled brightly. "I got word that I'm your new roommate permanently. Isn't that great news?"

"What about—"

"Don't worry about them," Vanessa snapped. "Come along."

Kate spent the next day trying to stay as far from Vanessa as she could and running over options to try and find out what happened to her friends. Nothing came to her. No plans, no brilliant insights. She ended up with nothing but a headache and an overwhelming desire to make this someone else's problem. It was just too big.

When at last the school day ended, it was pure delight to hide out in the journalism room discussing article ideas and format with the other students and with Miss Bernhardt's enthusiastic encouragement. The only black spot was Dean's conspicuous absence.

When the class was over, Katharine took her time packing up until the rest of the class had filed out.

"Sad to not see Jeannie today. I hope she's okay. I know you two are friends." Miss Bernhardt fixed the button on her gray cardigan.

Her statement was so unexpectedly in line with what was on her mind that Kate froze.

"Kate?"

"Can I talk to you?"

"Of course, Kate."

"Alright if I shut the door?"

Miss Bernhardt nodded and looked concerned.

Kate shut the door and sat at a small chair across the desk. She fidgeted. Unsure of where to begin.

"Is everything okay, Kate? You look troubled. Whatever it is, you can tell me. Then you and I can figure out what to do next."

Kate nodded, relieved to be there, to have made a decision,

to have someone else be responsible. "I think something bad happened to my friends." Her voice came out raspy and barely above a whisper.

Miss Bernhardt narrowed her eyes in concern and leaned forward.. "What do you mean? And which friends are you talking about?"

"JJ, uh Jennifer, Vanessa, and Jeannie. I'm sorry, I just real-ized I don't actually know their last names."

She gave her an encouraging smile. "Not to worry, the school isn't that big, I know who you're talking about. Do you mean someone hurt them somehow?"

Kate nodded frantically. "I don't know how to explain it. Va-nessa disappeared. For an entire day. And when she came back, she was... different. Like something was missing from her. She remembers things, but she doesn't act like herself at all. Then Jeannie and JJ disappeared. JJ's my roommate. It can't just be that we keep missing each other, or she got detention and I didn't hear. She should come back to the room eventually." Helpless, unwanted tears escaped her eyes and leaked down her cheeks. She rubbed at her face angrily.

"Disappeared? That is alarming."

"I think something bad happened to them. I think the school—or someone who works at the school, I mean, might have hurt them. I don't know what to do."

Miss Bernhardt reached across the table and squeezed her hand. "Thank you for telling me, Kate. I believe you."

"You do?"

"I do."

"What—what do we do?" Kate asked.

Miss Bernhardt stood and paced the room. "You don't need to do anything else. I'm so glad you told me. I'll handle things from here."

Kate breathed a sigh of relief. She'd done what she could for her friends. She turned to thank Miss Bernhardt when an arm wrapped around her throat, and a cloth was shoved into her face. Sickly sweet chemicals filled her nose, and she blacked out.

There was a too-familiar steel table and a shadowy figure with arms and legs that jerked like a marionette with broken strings. Then hands and hushed voices. Something sharper even than a scalpel cut into her, cut into things Kate had no words for. Taking her apart. Unspooling her into a dark, horrible nothingness.

Kate blinked against a bright flashing light. Her body hurt everywhere, as if she'd been rubbed raw from the inside out. That paralyzing, helpless feeling built in her chest and seemed to press heavier and heavier until she felt as if she'd merge with the cold steel table. But something flared up inside her. Anger. That thing she buried in liquor when Tanya dumped her. The thing that wanted to rage when her parents left her here, but she didn't dare let loose. She was afraid it would consume her and any chance she had at getting her life back.

This time she didn't bury it. She let it burn. Let it pull her to her feet.

The room she was in was small, windowless, and every inch was painted white but marred by creeping black mold. She was alone except for... a person didn't feel like the right word. But it was person-shaped. Like a white clay doll before someone sculpted and painted features and hair. As she watched, it raised one arm and stretched its stump of a hand. Fingers pulled apart, stringy as taffy.

She thought maybe she should scream, but all that came out was a strange, swallowed, choking squeak.

A similar noise, but dull and empty of actual feeling, echoed from its chest.

She took two steps back towards the wall and away from the thing. Several seconds later, it did the same. She stepped sideways, and the thing mimicked her, but faster this time.

As she stared in silence, it pulled apart its other hand to create fingers. Then split its feet into toes. It was changing color. Too slow for her to see it happen, but fast enough that it visibly no longer matched the white wall behind it, and instead was taking on a warm mix of pinks and light browns.

This was nuts. She turned and strode to the door and turned

to the knob. Locked, of course. But she jerked at it frantically and slammed her fist against the wall. "Hey, let me out of here!"

She startled at a thud and turned to see the thing imitating her gestures, but with no doorknob to grab, it was clutching at the empty air.

"Hey, let me out of here." Its voice was strange, airy, and high pitched like a strong wind whistling through trees.

Kate raised her right hand. The thing immediately raised its left, like it was her reflection in a mirror. She stepped towards it, and it stepped towards her. She stopped. It cocked its head to the side. She hadn't even realized she was doing that. She reached out a hand and touched her fingers to its outstretched hand. It was warm and soft. Not like clay at all, but not quite like skin either.

She hadn't seen it happen, but features had begun to form on its face. It had a still unformed, putty-like mouth, and dents that were turning brown like coffee soaking through a paper towel. Soon she was looking at a rough version of her own face.

"What are you?" she asked.

"What are you?" it echoed before she'd finished the sentence.

That strange weight still sat on her chest. She touched the skin above her sternum, and it moved nearly in time with her, a reflection only half a second behind. She was tired. God, she was so tired. It was like having the flu and every second she stood grew harder and harder. But somehow she didn't think it was a good idea to relax.

"I need to get out of here," they both said at the same time.

Kate walked towards the thing again, and it walked towards her. Its brown eyes were still dull and empty like doll eyes, but it had fingernails now. For some reason, the sight of its fingernails nauseated her. She put her palm flat against its chest. It was warm, soft, and a rhythmic thud pounded beneath the skin in time to her own heartbeat.

She shoved it.

It didn't budge under her hand but sent her flying across the room to land on her ass. As if a mocking parody of her, it jumped backward and clumsily dropped to the ground.

"Cool," it said.

"Cool," she said, sarcastically half a second behind it.

"Oh shit," it said.

"Oh shit," Kate said several seconds after it.

This was not good. Maybe no more talking. She had no idea what was happening. But this thing looked exactly like her now except for an emptiness behind the eyes.

"I think we're about done here," it said.

As if puppet strings were attached to her lips, Kate parroted. "I think we're about done here."

It smiled. Unwillingly, Kate smiled.

Her look-alike turned and walked to the door, knocked, and said, "I am complete. Let me out."

Kate turned, walked to a space opposite it, knocked on empty air, and said, "I am complete. Let me out."

Alone again, Kate involuntarily walked around the tiny room, running into the walls and the table, speaking nonsense words into the air. And every second, her body grew more tired, and her thoughts more distorted, as if someone were pulling them from her head with a straw.

The door opened, and her heart thumped hard in her chest. A familiar woman in a gray cardigan, her face temporarily masked by the bright lights streaming in from behind her, walked in. When she knelt in front of her, Kate recognized Miss Bernhardt. She tried to form her own words, to beg the woman to free her. But her mouth wouldn't move.

Her lips parted and closed, her jaw working, chewing on air. The next time her mouth opened, Miss Bernhardt slipped a soft, tasteless carrot between her teeth, and Kate's jaws continued working, unbidden. At the end, Miss Bernhardt tilted her head back and trickled water into her mouth. Her throat wouldn't move, and so the water dripped down her throat.

Miss Bernhardt patted her cheek fondly. "Everything is going to be fine now. You're being purified. I know it may not feel like it, but that's you up there just as surely as this body is also you. When we're done, you'll be free of all the feelings that used to torment you, that hurt those around you. This is a good thing, Katharine." She left, leaving Kate in darkness again.

Kate stood and moved as if tucking in and neatening her bed, then climbed into invisible blankets and lay down on the cold, white tile floor.

Whatever the thing attached to her was, it didn't sleep. She stared at the ceiling, eyes unblinking and dry. At some point, her brain shut down even if her eyes wouldn't close. Unwillingly, she stood and pantomimed, making her bed. She walked forward until she slammed into the wall and yet her legs continued moving as if they could carry her through stone. Her face banged and scraped against the wall, and her knees smashed until they were swollen with bruises, and at last, she sat down.

She raised her hand. "The green light is not literal, of course. It is symbolism for Gatsby's obsessions. With Daisy, money, status. The American Dream, if you will."

"Thank you, Miss Bernhardt," Kate said. The words kept pouring out of her mouth no matter what she did. The day continued that way. Words coming uncontrollable and contextless from her mouth, her body outside of her control walking, smiling, waving, and sitting.

Kate's mouth split into a painful smile that tugged at the dry, split corners of her lips. She reached out as if hugging someone.

"Thank you, Mother. Father. I'm so glad you're proud of me." Kate sat, and a wave of vertigo and nausea came over her.

"Oh, yes. School is wonderful. Thank you so much for sending me there. It's exactly what I've needed. I am so happy to see you and so excited and thankful to spend Christmas with you." She nodded her head and laughed. "I love you, too."

Kate was too tired for rage, but a cold, prickling anger wormed around in her guts. She couldn't know what her parents were saying, but it was pretty clear from the one side of the conversation that they were happy with this thing that had replaced her. This thing that was constantly sucking at her like a parasite that was stealing her life, and they liked it. When was the last time her parents had said they were proud of her? Hell, when had they last said they loved her? The last time she could remember them telling her either was when she was twelve years old and got the lead in a church Easter pageant. It wasn't long after that they grounded her for the first time for skipping youth group to hang out with her friends, catching frogs in the woods behind the church.

That heavy, familiar sorrow settled in her heart, forcing out her tired anger. If her parents liked this thing better, if they could love it in a way they couldn't love her, maybe she should just let it have her life. She'd made an absolute mess of it. Maybe this perfect, polite doppelganger of a monster deserved it more than she did.

Kate couldn't tell how long the thing that stole her face was away from school. But eventually, that horrible, churning vertigo happened again, and she determined the thing was in the car headed back to school. When the sensation ended, she pantomimed opening a car door and stood, smashing her face into the wall so hard she felt blood leak from her nose.

"I'm so sorry for all that I put you both through. I promise, from now on, I will be the daughter you always wanted." Kate stood in the dark, a broad smile on her face. "Yes, you're right, Father. I don't know how I became so lost. So confused. But I'm back, and I'll always be your little girl."

Hearing the words "I'll always be your little girl" echoing through the dark room drove her deepening depression back and reignited her rage, searing and overwhelming.

In her head, she screamed, "That's not me, that's not me! Why can't you tell that's not me?" over and over again while her body leaned forward for smiling hugs.

Then her body froze in mid-hug, and the words, "that's not me," rang and echoed through the small, dark room.

She stood straight. "I am so sorry, I don't know what came over me. I do feel a little carsick. I love you." Her face stretched into a strained grin. "You're right. Maybe it was a bit too soon to leave the school. But I'm back now. Goodbye. I love you both." She turned and walked, quickly hitting the opposite wall and continuing to slam into it as her body mimed walking.

It was a small thing, but for just one second, she'd had control.

The door opened behind her, and a sliver of light fell on the blank wall in front of her face.

"Kate? Holy shit, it is you."

She had expected it to be Miss Bernhardt or one of the other teachers with food, but it was Dean's face that peered down at her. She wanted to cry, to ask him how it was he was here, to beg him to take her out of here. But she couldn't move.

"I'm so sorry, Kate. I'm so sorry," he murmured. "We were going to bring you with us, but you disappeared before we could get to you. Then I saw that... thing, that other you, start freaking out, and I had to try. I'll explain everything later, we've got to go. Come on."

She had so many questions. Who was 'we,' how had he found her here, where had he gone? But she couldn't ask any of them.

"Come on, Kate." His voice was urgent, and he tugged her arm. "Kate? Say something. Can you walk?"

Her lips curved. "Yes, it was lovely to see my parents. I am glad to be back, though, thank you, Miss Bernhardt."

Dean flinched. "Fuck," he whispered. He looked deep in thought but finally seemed to reach a decision. "I have to believe this is really you somehow, and if you're here, so is Vanessa. So is Essie and all the others. They're here somewhere. Right now, though, I'm getting you out. I am sorry I can't ask your permission."

"I'll see you soon," Kate's mouth said.

Dean jumped. Kate could only experience one side of her doppelganger's conversations and actions, but could it see or hear what she was doing? It didn't seem to give a shit when it smashed her knees until they were bruised and swollen, or her face until her nose and lips bled.

It seemed Dean was thinking the same thing. "I'm sorry about this, Kate." He pulled off his t-shirt leaving just a white undershirt, and with some complicated folding and tucking, put the shirt over her head until it fit like a balaclava with the opening over her nose instead of her eyes. She could see a faint outline of the world through the black fabric as he hefted her over his shoulder. He wasn't much bigger than her, but was surprisingly strong and able to keep her helplessly moving legs from hitting him in the head and knocking them off balance.

Her lips moved, but the words were muffled against his back. His footsteps moved from the loud clacking of the wooden floors of the school, then he set her down. Her body began walking on its own, and his running footsteps came after her, hoisting her back over his shoulder. He lifted and wedged her through what felt like a window. Her back scraped against something sharp.

"Sorry again," he murmured.

She dropped through open air, landing hard and painfully on her left shoulder. The jolt rattled her teeth, and for a moment, her legs stopped moving. Then they started running.

There was a thump as Dean landed next to her. He gathered her back into his arms.

"Miss Bernhardt. There is an emergency on the second floor," Kate said.

Dean sucked his breath in sharply and started running, clumsy with the extra awkward weight of her body bouncing against his back and shoulder, and her traitorous legs' constant motion.

"Dean," someone hissed.

"Yeah. I got Kate." He set her down on the damp, cool ground. "There is something really wrong with her, though," he said.

A cool hand moved the shirt away from her face to reveal JJ. Relief and happiness threatened to overwhelm her. When had she come to think of these people as her friends and not just the people she hung out with by default at her new school? But they were. Not only that, they'd come for her when she screamed for help, even though no one else could or wanted to hear her.

"It is her. You were right. Hey, new girl," JJ said, her voice uncharacteristically serious and her eyes heavy with unshed tears.

Dean explained what he'd seen Kate do and say since finding her. "I can't explain it, but somehow she and that thing out there are tied together."

"The others?" JJ asked.

"I didn't see them. But Kate's was the only door I had time to get open. There were so many doors, JJ. They're probably all in there."

"Where, oh, where are you hiding?" Kate said. JJ and Dean jumped.

"Shit, cover her eyes. We don't know if it can see through her or not," Dean said.

Their faces disappeared behind the screen of black cotton.

"What do we do?" Dean asked.

"What we planned. We hike until we hit a road and then we hitch. It'll take longer having to carry Kate, but I think we can do it. Maybe if we get her far enough away from the school and that thing, it'll sever the connection between them."

"And maybe it won't. That thing went home with Kate's parents."

"Her parents live in the state. We go further. I don't fucking know, Dean. It's all I've got. If it works, we figure out a way to get the others out."

Dean was silent for what seemed a very long time. "Okay. You're right. It's the only idea we have." He grunted and heaved her back over his shoulder.

"We'll take care of you, Kate. You just fight hard to get that thing out of your head so that the real you can come back. Everything will be okay," JJ said.

Kate's head bounced against Dean's back, and her legs fought against the weight of JJ's arm, still trying to walk. Wind rustled the leaves, and somewhere an owl hooted, and JJ's command echoed through her head.

Her entire life was defined by fighting for the real Kate, and she was so goddamn tired. But this was the first time she'd had anyone fighting beside her. Maybe this time she'd win.

This House is Not Haunted

This house is not haunted. There are no ephemeral feet to pad down the halls in the deep dark of night, no mournful voices draping the air like gauze grotesquerie. If you wake slicked with sweat and the echoes of a scream on your lips, it is only nightmares. If you see a pair of eyes, blacker than black, a dark to suck the light and life from your soul, peering hungrily at you from the corners, you can be sure it is a trick of your imagination. No horrible sins are buried in the basement or mummified in the attic. This home is ever wholesome, burdened only with an excess of shadow and drafty windows. There is no click of fingernails on the windows, no familiar voices of the departed whispering your name, beckoning you to follow deeper and deeper into an impossible hole in the world. Nothing waits for you to close your eyes. Rest.

This house is not haunted.

– Excerpt from the journal of Robert James Boyd III, 1894

I considered killing the little girl immediately. It would be so easy to lure her up the stairs into the bedroom painted palest yellow with the most resplendent dollhouse towering over piles of dollies, crayons, and a rainbow of construction paper. It would be even easier to shove her out the window that overlooked the driveway below, crude as that would be. Sudden, random violence brings its own pleasures. Screams and splatters and sirens.

I could steal her mother's voice and whisper the girl's name until she followed me outside, where I would bury her in peat until she dried and leathered. A companion to share my big empty house. Or I could plant my own seed deep in her ear and send her home to grow rotten and malignant from the inside out.

All these things that would be so *fun*, but something stopped me. Perhaps it was the years of boredom while this house stood empty, its reputation too fearsome to tempt even the bargain hunters. My only company drunken teenagers and, equally dull and stupid, ghost hunters. Instead, I crept behind her while she clutched tight to her mother's hand, the woman distracted by the enthusiasm of the real estate agent.

The woman was entranced by the bay window, the vaulted ceilings, the stone fireplace. Lumbering behind them was the girl's father. He looked bored, distracted, but wandered off every now and again to test an appliance and make approving sounds. I gathered from their conversation that this was not the first house they had looked at today.

Yes, it might be nice to have a family again. Bright and sunny people to bring laughter and life to the house. Someone to toy with until I grew bored, until I found that perfect thing to destroy them so completely.

So, I waited, quiet as can be, in the shadows while they toured. The little girl's shy disposition turned slowly to gregarious enthusiasm as the tour continued. I allowed her a glimpse of my hand, beckoning from the shadows. But just for a second, not long enough for her to be sure of what she saw. She paled and glanced nervously in my direction but said nothing. That was good. A good child. A quiet child. A child whose first impulse was not to shout in alarm was the best kind of child.

Yes, they would do nicely.

Molly cried on and off the entire day her family moved into the lovely old house that was perched alone at the end of a sprawling, gravel driveway. It was built on an artificial hill that sloped down into a wet, pungent bog, and it was beautiful. The sturdy red bricks, pure white pillars framing the door, and lush flower gardens stood out deliciously against the backdrop of green and brown. And she hated it with every ounce of her six-year-old body. It was wrong, bad in a way she couldn't put into words. The shadows made shapes like hands and moved when they should not. And to make matters worse, the stress of moving was making her parents argue even more than they usually did, which made them even more impatient with her.

She wanted to go home. But home was on the other side of an entire ocean. They assured her this would be home soon enough. That this would even be better than home. Far away from the busy city and the pressure to work harder, faster, make more money. Here they would be closer to her grandmother, who was nothing but a warm brogue on the end of the phone to her, and best of all, they could "focus on each other" and save a crumbling marriage. Molly didn't know what any of that meant, of course, only that it shouldn't mean even more snapping at each other and even more ignoring her, but it did.

Life had already taught her that while her parents loved her, they did not care about her opinion or her feelings. And so, she learned to keep her opinions, and her feelings, to herself.

"Why don't you go play in your new room?" her mother suggested.

Molly didn't want to leave her, didn't want to be alone in this strange new house, but her mother often cast her orders as suggestions, so she knew there would be no arguing with this one. The stairs were the same warm, golden-brown wood as the rest of the floors, with a ribbon of plush red carpet up the middle. She imagined herself as a princess as she ascended the stairs, her hand gripping the ornate banister that loomed above her head.

The movers had already brought her bed and dressers up but had not yet gotten to the boxes marked as hers. The resplendent dollhouse that had been here when they looked at the house had gone with the real estate agent, so there was nothing much to do except take off her shoes and slide across the wood floors in stockinged feet. Back and forth she went, until after a while she forgot how much she hated the creepy old house and giggled as she slipped across the floor and crashed harmlessly into the side of her bed.

"Molly." Her name was whispered from the shadows. A dry, dusty sound like a fall wind through dead leaves and a strange, wet, earthy smell filled the room.

She froze, half on and half off her bed. "Who's there?"

"Molly." The voice rustled through the cobwebs and the dust bunnies and seemed to come from everywhere and nowhere all at once.

"Mommy?" the little girl's lip quivered.

"Will you be my friend, Molly?"

The girl stood and raced down the stairs. She clung to her mother's leg until the woman, afraid of dropping a box on the little girl, snapped at her to move.

"There's no one in your room, Molly. Please let Mommy and Daddy work right now. If you promise to stay out of the way and on the couch, you may stay downstairs, okay?" She returned to carrying boxes and rearranging furniture without another word or even a glance.

Molly went to the couch and sat, folded in on herself with her knees under her chin, and her arms wrapped around her shins. She watched the chaos of moving through teary eyes, fear, and petulant hurt fighting a war in her heart. It would serve them right if she went back to her room and got eaten. But, she didn't want to get eaten, so she stayed, sad and quiet amidst the neglectful bustle.

The game I played with my little family grew dull more quickly than I hoped. It did not take long for the little girl to stop telling her parents about the shadows that moved, the voice that called her into the dark, or the small, leathered fingers that found her own hands in the darkness and held them tight. They called me her "invisible friend" and teased her until she learned not to talk about me. It was lovely, the slow destruction of a child. The narrowing of all that potential into something small and fearful.

But, I was still getting bored. I couldn't hurt the little girl, not yet, not while she was so ripe for further games. So, I let her be for a night. Let her sleep deep and undisturbed. That peace would haunt her later, I hoped.

The woman was also important to my game. Her disbelief, her rationalizations, they were the most delectable seasoning to my own little torments. The man, on the other hand, well, he was just superfluous. All the disbelief and unintentionally cruel jokes about invisible friends, but only half the sting in the girl's eyes.

He fancied himself handy around the house. The man from another of my families, a full century or more ago, had been like that. Always hammering and sawing away, an air of benign disinterest while his little boy slipped deeper and deeper into my company. Such men moved through the world with an assumption that they were safe and so made very easy targets. After the girl was asleep and her parents began their nightly ritual of picking at one another in hushed voices, I curled up in the shadows, and I knocked.

"What was that?" the woman asked.

"Sounds like it came from the basement."

"I've a load of laundry going, probably that."

I knocked again, twice.

"I'll go check it out. Might be something out of alignment." The relief at being able to escape the brewing argument was evident in the man's voice. He threw a bathrobe over his pajamas, grabbed his toolbox, and descended the stairs.

As he examined the washer and dryer, waiting to hear my knock again, I struck him across the back of the head so that he slumped to the ground unconscious. I placed my hand over his mouth until every bit of his voice rested in my palm like a quivering mouse. I swallowed it and then called up the stairs, "Got a bit of work to do. Go ahead and go to bed."

Upstairs the woman sighed dramatically and closed the bedroom door.

I tied the man up and perched atop his chest and waited for him to wake up. When he did, he opened his mouth wide enough for me to see his tonsils. He was, of course, trying to scream, but to no avail, as his voice had joined the dozens of others that belonged to me.

"We are going to have so much fun," I said, still using his voice.

His eyes widened, and he thrashed about like a fish. I giggled and slowly filled his gaping, silent mouth with spiderwebs. Oh, yes, this was great fun. It was exactly what I needed. I blew spores into his nose until mushrooms took root and began to grow. Soon he couldn't breathe through his mouth or nose, and all too quickly, he was dead.

I sighed in disappointment. I'd been overexcited. But, perhaps we could have more fun one day. So, I dragged him outside and buried him deep in the bog with all the rest of my families. Let him leather and brown until he was just like me.

Molly's insistence that a monster killed her daddy and that he still whispered to her in the dark of night led to her first round of therapy. Just when she learned to lie and say that he must have run off like everyone said (after all, her parents were quite obviously unhappy), her daddy began to visit her at night. Dried and thin, as if the bones had disintegrated beneath his browned, leathered skin. But enough of his features were so perfectly preserved that there was no doubt it was him. His distinct, angular nose and sharp cheekbones remained prominent in a face otherwise flattened and shriveled. His too-short fingernails were preserved so perfectly it was uncanny, and his hair was dirty and uncharacteristically messy, but still ginger with gray seeping in from the temples. He stood over her bed, silent as a statue, smelling of peat, and so very alien.

When he visited, the voice from the shadows would go quiet for a little while. Then it would giggle and whisper mean, cruel things. Things she thought sometimes but never said aloud. Things about her parents. Things about herself. She plugged her ears, but it did nothing to mute the voice. She wondered if maybe her therapist was right. That the things she heard and saw were inside her own head, products of her own imagination. But then that dry hand would rasp down her arm in a parody of a caress and clutch at her fingers, and she couldn't deny to herself that this was really happening.

Her withdrawn quiet, the way she lashed out when

startled, led to her second round of therapy and the development of an almost preternatural ability to smile through anything. Even when her pet hamster disappeared and then returned, a nightmare like a desiccated potato scuttling about her bedroom floor in the dark. Even when her first and only sleepover ended in her friend's disappearance and her voice was added to the chorus that whispered to her from the shadows, and even when the grandmother they'd crossed an ocean to be near collapsed and drowned in the peat bog behind the house during the little girl's birthday party, Molly kept on smiling.

I became aware that Molly was making plans to escape sometime after her eighteenth birthday. We'd been together for more than ten years, and I admit, I was quite angry that she thought she could leave me now after all the time I'd invested in our family.

As she lay in bed, I wore her father's voice and asked her why she wanted to leave me. I wore her grandmother's voice and begged her to stay while they both stood, silent sentinels at the foot of her bed. I wore my own voice when I asked her what would happen to her mother if she left. Finally, I was gratified to hear her break the silence with a choked sob.

Still, she plotted her escape. Her grades were not good enough for college, and she hadn't been able to hold down a job to save money. All those sleepless nights were rough on the grade point average and work attendance, so much to my delight, her future and her options were narrowing further and further. She even tried finding men on the internet who would take her away in exchange for sex, but it didn't take many whispers in her mother's ears before even those avenues closed.

"You're not going anywhere, my sweet, smilin' Molly," I sang to her from the shadows, night after night until boredom began to creep back in. I wasn't ready to let Molly go yet. But, soon, her mother wouldn't be necessary.

I waited as long as I could, but when I discovered that the woman intended to send her daughter away, to rent her an apartment in the city to try and force her to support herself, I knew I could wait no longer. When she took her sleeping pills and went to bed, I perched atop her chest and whispered nightmares into her ears until they bled. Then I pulled out her eyes and filled the sockets with yellow flower petals, before I stole her voice and buried her alive, deep in the bog. So deep, it would take her years to dig herself out after the bog left her shriveled, leathered, and then re-animated her. It was what she deserved, trying to take the girl away from me.

The thing killed Molly's mother on her nineteenth birthday. She and Molly had fought. Her mother demanded to know what happened, why her daughter had become such a loser, a mooch. That it wasn't the example her parents set. Well, to say that they fought wasn't quite right, though that was how she and her mother both thought of it. Molly said nothing during this tirade. She didn't say much of anything anymore. She smiled, and she nodded and said, please, thank you, hmm, yes, no in all the right places. But otherwise, she'd grown quiet.

Molly had known it would happen eventually. She didn't know why, but the thing that lived in her house wanted her alone. So, when she came down the stairs for breakfast, and her mother wasn't working at her computer as she usually was, it did not come as a surprise when her voice joined the others that spoke to her, cajoled her, summoned her from the shadows. She didn't join the others in standing at the foot of her bed at night, and she was unsure if that would have brought her comfort. She could pretend her mother had run away like everyone said her father did.

She reported her mother missing, but kept her mouth shut about what she thought happened to her. She had learned her lesson about honesty. There would be an investigation, but it would take years to have her mother de-

clared dead and activate the terms of her will. So, she resigned herself to the house and the thing she shared it with.
Eventually, she found a job she could do as a stay-at-home
telemarketer. It didn't pay enough to leave, but was enough
to feed herself. Eventually, though, she couldn't afford the
substantial utility bills on the large house and put her final paycheck into canned beans and vegetables before the
power was turned off.

"Will you be my friend now, Molly?" I asked. Molly had
become an adult, I realized. She was tall and full-hipped,
no longer 'the little girl.' I was unsure how I felt about that.
Adults were so dull. Their potential was worn out or com-
mitted, and so the paths before them were so easily narrowed, so easily obliterated.

I didn't see any path for Molly that didn't end with her buried amongst my collection in the bog. She would never leave
this house, and that meant she was growing boring. There was
nothing left to destroy, nothing left to take from her, no surprises
waiting for me. The time to kill her was coming soon. I did not
look forward to the long years alone, waiting for a new family to
move in. Perhaps that stayed my hand longer than it should have.

She lay silently in bed for longer and longer stretches of time.
She didn't move into her parent's bedroom, but she did eventually take over their bedding and created herself a canopy with the
sheets that I was forced to tear down every night to reach her. It
was mildly annoying, and I didn't understand the point, but she
seemed to like creating mild annoyance. It was cute.

"Shut up. You're not real," she answered from beneath her
fort of sheets, still smiling blankly and pleasantly at the ceiling.

I laughed. "What are you saying, smilin' Molly?"

"You are not real. This house is not haunted. I have a problem."

I reached through the hanging sheets and caressed her hand.
"Doesn't this feel real?" I asked, using her mother's voice.

"You are not real. This house is not haunted. I have a problem," she repeated.

"You can say that as often as you like, I'm not going anywhere, and neither are you."

Her mask of a smile twisted into something I couldn't read. Something with an ugly kind of mirth. "I know."

That smile sparked my curiosity for the first time since before I'd killed her mother, and it stayed my killing hand for yet another night.

Molly looked into her future, and she saw nothing. An early death at best, whether at her own hand or the monster's. At worst, an endless stream of days blurring together with no one and nothing except for voices whispering in the night. But her mother's death had ignited something. It started out small, but it was growing. It wasn't hope exactly, but some vengeful, desperate cousin that urged action. She literally had nothing left to lose, and no one to answer to for her actions. There was a freeing, dark exhilaration in that lack of any meaningful consequences.

While the sun was high, she prepared. Her father, who she only remembered as a tall, gruff figure with his head shoved under the sink or hammering away at something he had no patience to explain, had maintained an extensive collection of tools and supplies for his many home repair projects. Stacked in the corner of the basement were several cans of unopened paint thinner. She pried the lid off one, coughing from the horrid, chemical fumes, and then climbed the stairs back up to her bedroom and waited until nightfall.

I slipped through the darkness, skipping over the splotches of dim moonlight that leaked in through the windows to dance with the shadows. When I reached Molly's bedroom, something was different. Her breath was not the deep, even sound of sleep or the hushed, frustrated sound of insomnia. It was short, shallow, and sharp, as if she were out of breath and wanted to pant but was trying to be quiet. She'd breathed that way before she futilely stabbed me with a steak knife as a teenager.

The floor was slick with something that peeled the varnish from the wood. Curiosity piqued, I entered her room cautiously, pulling out the voices of all those I'd taken from her and used them all like a choir to ask, "What game are we playing tonight, smilin' Molly?"

She sat up at the end of the bed and peered into the dark. Her grin was wide, wicked, and without humor. "A new one." She flicked her wrist, and something scraped and hissed, and a tiny flame appeared between her fingers. She let the match burn for just a second and then tossed it.

The match arced towards the chemical coated ground. Just before it landed, I blew a gust of damp, boggy air from my hollow chest, and the flame died.

Molly shrieked and leaped from the bed, hands extended like claws, and threw herself into the shadows at me. I skipped easily out of her reach. She fell on her stomach, and the air whooshed from her lungs. I skipped over to her and sat on her back, pinning her to the floor like a butterfly in a collection.

"Well, well, Molly. What an excellent game. So unpredictable." Truly, it was the first time she'd interested me in quite a while. I'd thought I'd tormented every bit of rebelliousness from her and obliterated every future version of her until her only path forward was quiet, miserable death. But here she was, hatching plots to kill me.

"Just kill me already," she shouted through clenched teeth.

"Why would I do that when you're finally willing to play with me? I can't wait to see what you do tomorrow night. We are going to have so much fun," I said.

This house is not haunted. I hope that if I say it's not real often enough, it will become true. Like Tinkerbell. If I say I don't believe, maybe it will die. But no matter what I do, it doesn't. I've stabbed it, tried to light it on fire, struck it with an axe until its hand fell off. The hand just clawed the ground and the air like a living beast until it returned, undamaged, to its master.

It ran away with the axe, and the following night, it held my arm against the nightstand and chopped off my pinkie, giggling the entire time. Like it was a game. Chop chop, tag, you're it. I don't think it wants to kill me. In the winter, it sometimes even starts a fire in the hearth for me. It says we're family. I guess we are. If I won, if I killed it, I don't know what I would even be anymore. I don't have a place in the world outside this house.

In its way, I think it needs me too. What is family, after all, if not the people who give you purpose?

–Excerpt from the journal of Molly McPherson, date unknown

Karaoke

A few drunken, mocking stanzas of your old high school fight song sung on the sidewalk outside my door and...
There's something about you.
Come inside.
I've built a stage, just for you.

1. DON'T STOP BELIEVIN'

"Karaoke, seriously?" Paige says.

"Yes, seriously. Come on, we used to do it all the time in high school. What's a reunion without reliving the goofy shit you used to do?" Kelsey holds the door open, her hand leaving smears in the thick coat of grease and dust coating the glass.

"Never here, though. Hasn't this place been closed since like, disco was cool?" you say.

Kelsey shrugs. "It's open now."

Flashing lights and guitar power chords leak out of the building. No one is on the stage, but a handful of people sit at the bar, getting drunk enough to be the first.

You laugh. "You know what? Fuck it. Let's do this."

Paige raises one skeptical eyebrow at you. Since Jess and Kelsey left, it has been just the two of you. Bored, broke, and constantly scrounging for work in this dying shithole of a town. Unlike you, her parents don't make her pay rent while she pursues her passion, which is posting surreal, digital horror art to

DeviantArt and trying to sell prints on Etsy. On the rare occasion she manages to sell something, she gets to keep the money for herself. She knows just how little you can afford a night out drinking and paying too much money for corn chips soaked in congealed nacho cheese. But she shrugs as if to say, "your funeral."

You follow Kelsey inside, and Paige and Jess trail you with slow reluctance.

Once inside, Jess makes a beeline for the bar, her glossy, blonde hair reflecting the silver spots of the mirror ball spinning above.

Just as you're about to settle into a table that doesn't wobble on loose screws and uneven legs quite as much as the others, Jess grabs your elbow.

"Fuck singing with a bunch of drunk old people. If we're going to do this, we're going to do it right. I got us a room." Jess holds up a key.

You feel a fleeting flash of resentment at the knowledge that she probably paid for it on her parents' credit card, but still, you grin in relief. You were a little tipsy from the margaritas at dinner but hadn't been looking forward to getting up in front of strangers, even if the total number of staff and other patrons was less than twenty. "What do we owe you?"

Jess waves a hand. "Nothing. Whatever. I'm an actress, right? A shitty stage is still a stage. Maybe I can call it a business expense on my taxes."

"Do you even make enough to have to file taxes?" Paige asks, the corners of her lips arched in a barely concealed smile.

The barb strikes home. Jess deflates.

Her sorrowful face makes you feel even worse about your own unkind thoughts, so you clear your throat and drape an arm over Jess's shoulder. "Thanks for the upgrade. This'll be fun."

There's no elevator, and the stairs are a baffling zig-zag of clanking metal steps that look very much like a design afterthought. The room is on the third floor, and the stairs are steep, but Kelsey bounds past you, apparently still in shape even after her soccer career ended at college graduation. She probably still runs every morning and does something like co-ed rugby on the weekends.

Jess opens the flimsy wooden door into a room that looks like a time capsule. It had hideous orange shag carpet, gold flecks in the ceiling, and a three-inch-tall stage of wood laminate, bubbled and distorted from moisture.

"Well, this is, um…" Jess's voice trails off.

"A disgusting pit of mildew and poor design choices that is almost definitely haunted by a ghost who wears a jumpsuit and knows every line and dance move from *Saturday Night Fever*?" Paige offers.

"It's retro," you say, trying not to laugh at Jess's horrified face.

Kelsey gives the room a skeptical appraisal. "Whatever this is, it requires beer. Be right back."

When she returns, you settle in at the small, round, yellow-tinged table and pour beer from the pitcher into four red cups. The beer is exactly what you expected. Thin-tasting, room temperature, and nearly flat.

"Phones in the bag, ladies." Paige holds out an olive green messenger bag adorned with patches and pins.

You and the others toss them in without complaint, but Jess hesitates.

"Sorry, Jess. Your social media fans will survive one night of not seeing literally every single thing you do. First rule of karaoke night: no worries about finding yourself on the internet tomorrow morning. Phone. In. The. Bag."

"Second rule of karaoke, beer." Kelsey raises a cup. "Fuck getting all sentimental and shit, but I've missed us all being together the past few years. So, to old friends." You all clink your cups together.

You sit and chat, and though you mostly stay quiet, you enjoy hearing your friends' stories of mishaps and triumphs as the alcohol breaks down the barriers that time and distance put up. Jess tells you about going to auditions and the time she showed up in her own high school cheer uniform, and a casting director told her she wasn't a believable cheerleader. Kelsey confirms your guess and talks about her co-ed rugby team, and the time she gave the guy she was crushing on a concussion by accident during practice. Paige complains about people wanting art of their *Dungeons and Dragons* characters and then getting mad about her prices. And you? Well, it takes more beer for you to talk, but eventually, you admit to checking out community college tuition rates and finding even that too expensive.

Perhaps to prevent you all from getting sucked into melancholy, Jess stands abruptly. "Well, let's get this shit started. I call the first song." She grabs the mic and strikes a sultry, model pose on the stage.

Even if you didn't know Jess, you could guess what her karaoke song would be. One look at her conspicuously designer clothes, artful no-makeup-looking makeup, and gym toned-but-not-too-muscular body, and you knew it would be something popular, dramatic, and indulgent. So, when Journey strums out those first few famous notes, you shake your head, groan, and are not surprised. But you're different from the others. You're kind. You don't heckle her. Even though you know she's the quintessential big fish in a small pond who jumped into the ocean that was LA. You know her parents are bankrolling a doomed attempt at becoming an actress, and Jess will eventually give up and marry some guy with money, and you'll all probably never see her again.

"Journey sucks!" Paige hollers and tosses an empty solo cup at the little stage.

"Hold on to that feeling," Jess croons and seamlessly adds, "and I paid for the upgrade to the private room, bitches, so shut up and let me sing."

You laugh and fill your cup again. Singing in front of people makes you nervous, and you're drinking more than you should.

Jess ends with a flourish, and you all clap, cheer, boo, and jeer in turn. She bows and throws the empty solo cup Paige tossed back at her. It falls so short of hitting Paige that it starts everyone laughing.

You're so close. Close enough to touch. You smell like beer and sweat and a broken heart. Just like this place. Just like me.

You must hear my heart pounding through the air ducts. You don't look at me. I'm a little disappointed. But you will see me. Eventually.

2. EYE OF THE TIGER

Kelsey snatches the microphone. As the notes of Survivor's classic song begins, Kelsey bobs her head along with the beat.

Anyone else in your little group would get shit for picking a song even worse than Jess's, but Kelsey has a temper. And calves the size of small trees. Also, her rugby crush was not the first time she'd given someone a concussion or broken a nose or split a lip. All that was in the course of sports, but none of you are as comfortable with violence and aggression as she is, and even if you won't say it, she scares you a little.

The video loops behind Kelsey, reflecting its flashing neon colors on her orange hair. A black and white image flashes on the screen. It's jarring and distorted like someone put a shitty Instagram filter over it. But it's your face. You open your mouth to say something, but the image disappears, replaced by a screaming crowd and Survivor's lyrics. You shake your head. Karaoke videos are weird. It was a random shot of some random person who happened to look kind of like you.

Maybe it's the alcohol or the startling image or the nostalgia of seeing old friends. But you find yourself dipping into melancholy. Imagining life if, like Jess and Kelsey, you were just here for a visit. Not another Friday night in the place you spent all your Friday nights. Jess and Kelsey managed to get out of this crap town. And for whatever reason, Paige likes it here. She says it's good inspiration, whatever that means. You think maybe she's just comfortable.

But you hate it and never had a chance for anything else. Not a pretty, blonde, all-American girl cheerleader with rich parents like Jess. Not athletic like Kelsey, with her soccer scholarship that at least got her a degree and a shitty office job in Cleveland. Not smart enough to get into a college worth going into debt for. You organized this night because you deserved it. One night of frivolity and pretending you were still a teenager who thought the world was going to open wide for her as soon as she walked across that graduation stage.

You stand abruptly. That train of thought was one quick dive into spending the entire night with your friends being a wet blanket of depression. "We need more beer. I'll call."

"I can get this round," Paige says. You love and despise her for saving you from yourself and your increasing credit card debt. She picks up the olive green phone on the wall and tugs on the corkscrew cord a few times in amusement. With an expression of mock confusion and shock, she marvels at the oversized buttons. "Why, what is this thing? It's like a phone, but plugged into the wall? What ancient, primitive people used this mysterious object?"

You laugh and feel the creeping sadness melt away.

"Actually, remind me to take a picture of this place before we go. I've got a killer idea to draw." She puts the receiver to her ear and waits. At last, she frowns and hangs up. "No answer. Must be busted. Anybody desperate enough yet to climb those stairs again?"

"I'll go," Kelsey says. She hands you the mic.

Can you see me, yet? You're so close. I feel as though I'm singing my heart out to you, and all you hear are whispers on the breeze.

3. WHERE THE WILD ROSES GROW

You're anxious. You could use some more beer before singing.

Paige drapes an arm over your shoulder. "How about a duet?"

You've always been the quiet one in your group. But also its center. The ear to listen when someone needs to vent and the shoulder everyone cries on. The one who keeps everyone else's secrets and helps carry everyone's pain. In high school, you were the one who kept popular, cheerleader Jess hanging out with a group of misfits, at least when no one was looking. The one who gave Kelsey a reason to hang out with anyone besides her jock friends, who she never felt comfortable being weak in front of.

But Paige has always been there, a constant shadow holding a sketchbook. She latched onto you like a barnacle in the second grade and never let go. Sometimes it was annoying. Like when she copied your blunt bangs and combat boot style in high school, or when she showed up when you were out with the other waitresses at your last job because she was bored and lonely. But she was your best friend. You loved her. And in this second, you loved her even more for saving you from singing solo.

You lean into her, grinning widely. "Fuck yeah. Let's throw some creepy into all this retro pop ballad shit."

"You wanna be Nick or Kylie?" she asks.

You know exactly what she means and grin wickedly. "I call Nick."

Paige swoons against the wall. "Fine, I shall be the Wild Rose."

You and Paige dance together in a dramatic, clumsy waltz while The Bad Seeds begin playing.

On the screen, Nick Cave vamps pale and dramatic, and Kylie floats dead and serene. The video blinks out, and you're staring at your own stunned face looking at the monitor in a karaoke parlor. The image blinks, and it's you at the kitchen table with your parents. The video doesn't have audio, but you remember this dinner from last year, when you got into a fight because they just couldn't understand why your jobs cleaning rich people's summer vacation homes and waiting tables wasn't enough for you to move out. It blinks again, and it's a younger you, looking eagerly into the mailbox for any news on your college applications.

It feels like the video is trying to gain your trust by showing you things you know are true.

You point. "Do you see that?"

Paige opens her eyes and draws herself up from her melodramatic death swoon, and Jess winces guiltily and shoves her phone back into the messenger bag.

"See what?" Jess asks.

Paige shoots her a dirty look and hops off the stage, grabs the bag, and moves it further away.

"I'm waiting on a callback. I just needed to check." Jess sticks out her lip in a pout.

"You didn't see, umm, me? On the screen just now?" you say.

Paige gapes at you. "No. Uh, you okay, Abby?"

You rub your temples. "You really didn't see it?"

"I didn't see anything weird. I mean, anything weirder than typical karaoke video shit, anyway. You okay?" Paige repeats.

You force a smile. "Yeah. You're right. Karaoke videos are weird."

The door opens, and you jump, but it's only Kelsey.

"Hey, did, uhh, anybody check what time this place closes?" Kelsey asks.

"No. But, I mean, it's Friday. So. Late, probably. Why?" Jess asks.

"Well, there's nobody down there. It looks like they closed up," Kelsey says.

"They wouldn't close with people still inside," you say.

Kelsey shrugs. "I don't know. Probably made an announcement, but the speaker system looks as old as everything else. Probably busted in our room, so we didn't hear it."

It's too much weird shit. "I need to pee."

"And I need to see for myself," Jess says.

You step outside, and Jess turns towards the stairs while you turn towards the bathroom sign. Inside, you let out a breath and stare at your face in the mirror. "It's fine. You're fine," you tell the reflection. You turn on the water, and it leaks out in a thin stream. You cup your hands and scoop the rust tinged water between your palms and toss it on your face. The cool water clears your head and calms the beating of your heart.

With a pop, the television in the corner of the room turns on. There's no sound, but it looks like a music video from the '80s. A man with long hair and a white, puffy shirt sings, his hand clutching his chest. Your lips curve in a smile at the cheesiness, but then the video cuts out.

Jess' face blinks onto the screen. Jess is in high school, leaning in to whisper to a more popular girl whose name you can't remember anymore. There is no audio, but when the young version of you walks past, they cover their mouths to hide their laughter. It's all too obvious who, if not what, they were talking about.

The scene repeats in different places, Jess whispering to different girls, over and over. You, oblivious, walking away with laughter at your back.

You lean against the counter. What you're looking at is impossible. But you can't deny that it's Jess. Every detail from her high, blonde ponytail to her pleated cheerleader skirt was perfect. But more than that, it explained something about high school you'd never understood. How you went, for years, from being an invisible nobody, someone people thought of as nice enough when they thought of you at all, to a target for gossip and too-close-to-home insults.

What are you going to say to Jess? She can't possibly believe you saw old videos of her on a karaoke bathroom TV. And does it matter, really? High school left scars, no doubt, but it's over. Years over. What can she say to you except, "Sorry, I was a shit when I was sixteen"? You gaze at the screen again, but it's gone dark. If you say something, you're just going to sound crazy. Drunk and paranoid and even resentful.

"Pull it the fuck together, Abby," you whisper to your pallid reflection in the water spotted mirror. You leave the bathroom. The only lights in the hall are the dim, buzzing emergency lights, and you strain your eyes to see the numbers on the doors.

A strangled scream makes you jump. It came from below. You race to the stairs and lean over the railing.

At the bottom of the stairs is Jess. Her head turned at an impossible angle to stare right at you. A thin trickle of blood leaks from her lips. Behind her, a television screen plays a grainy black and white video. It's a video of a younger version of you. You're sitting next to Paige, egging her on while she draws rude cartoons of Jess fucking various football players. Your face burns with shame and embarrassment at this reminder of your own youthful, cruel, and petty jealousy. The feelings make you freeze on the stairs, staring at the screen until it turns black, releasing you from its clutches.

You run down the steep stairs so fast it's a miracle you don't

fall.

"Jess?" You shake her, and her head lolls so far to the side you think it's going to fall off. Impossible, but you scream and drop her anyway.

You know what it's like to be trapped. You know what it's like to be abandoned by your friends. But you don't know yet that you're completely alone.

You've always been alone.

4. YOU OUGHTA KNOW

"I'll go get our phones," Paige whispers, as if afraid to wake her.

You stare at the body of your friend who you've known for so long and were so angry with minutes ago. You glance at the screen again, afraid that it's going to turn back on and show you something else horrible about your friends. Or worse, about yourself. But it stays blessedly dark.

Footsteps click-clack down the hall, and Paige appears at the top of the stairs. "Our phones are gone."

It takes you a moment to pull your eyes away from Jess to look at Paige and process what she just said. "What do you mean? You collected them. Where could they have gone?"

Paige is pale, and a thin sheen of sweat threatens to flush her thick black eyeliner and mascara off her eyes and onto her cheeks. "Jess really wanted hers. Maybe she took them?" She looks down, refusing to meet your eyes as if the suggestion were a betrayal.

"She doesn't have the bag with her." Kelsey waves at Jess.

"Maybe she dropped it," Paige says.

"You want to go hunting for it?" Kelsey asks, a hard edge to her voice.

Paige opens her mouth but closes it and shakes her head.

You stand and clear your throat. "Okay. We just need to

leave. We'll go outside and wave someone down and call 911."

The others nod, and you start to go down the stairs, but Kelsey pushes past, leading the way down the three flights of stairs to the main bar. It's not closed, not like you expect. The chairs aren't up on tables for the cleaning staff. There are still cups and plates on the tables. Upon closer inspection, the fries are shriveled and dry, and the nachos are covered in a thick layer of green mold. Dust coats everything like dingy frost.

What you're looking at is impossible, but there's no time to ponder this new, maddening mystery. You yank on the front door. It's locked, and where there should be a bolt is a mound of melted, twisted metal. You go to the bar, the others watching you as if you might be a dangerous animal. You ignore them and find a corkscrew. The image of Jess and her betrayals, and of you and yours, are so fresh in your mind. A rush of rage and self-loathing comes over you, and you slam the tip into the glass as hard as you can. It makes a satisfying, crisp snick, but doesn't shatter or explode into shards the way you want. All it leaves behind is a chip the size of a pinhead. You bash it against the glass again, but it's as if the glass is ready for you now, and you can't even do that much damage again.

Paige puts a hand on your shoulder. "Abby." Her voice is soft and even, the way you talk to an angry drunk when you're waiting tables. You shove her off but start to calm down despite yourself.

Kelsey stares at you for a moment as if she's never seen you before. She clears her throat. "Okay. There must be a phone down here, right?"

The three of you search the bar for a phone. There's only an empty jack where it should be.

"What are we going to do? What the fuck is going on?" Paige says.

"Let's check some of the other rooms. Maybe someone left their phone by accident," you suggest.

You turn and climb to the second floor, careful not to look up to see Jess's body on the landing just above. The blue track lighting in the floor turns your shadows into huge, monstrous shapes slumping across the ceiling.

The rooms are empty, and when you open the doors, the odor of mildew suggests they've not been opened in quite some time. At the site of one of the screens, the memory of your own face, of Jess, flashing across a screen like that makes you freeze. Staring. Waiting for it to turn on. But it stays blessedly dark.

"Did you see anything? When she—" Paige's voice trails off.

For a moment, you think she's talking about what you saw on the screen. But she means Jess. When Jess fell. Fuck, when she *died*. "No. We went different directions. I heard her scream, and I ran."

Kelsey shoves by. She strides down the hall, slamming doors open, blundering through each room as if bluster and squared shoulders would let her take charge of... whatever this was. You follow. Too shocked to be annoyed. But Paige rolls her eyes and starts checking rooms on the other side of the hallway. Kelsey slams open the door at the end of the hall, and the screen crackles to life.

You try to pull the door closed, but Kelsey is stronger than you and holds it open, staring at the screen as if entranced.

"What are you doing? No one has been in that room since before cell phones were even invented," you say.

You close your eyes briefly and offer a silent prayer that whatever appears on that screen is innocuous. An electrical glitch turning on the TV to play an innocuous karaoke video.

Kelsey's face appears, plastered on the screen floor to ceiling. You draw in a breath.

Her own heavy breathing stops. "What?"

Kelsey sits in an office chair wearing a shitty polyester suit and boots. She's typing. On the screen is an email with the subject line, "Re: Applicant used you for a reference, thoughts?"

You go rigid. You think your heart even stops beating for a second. You remember this. You spotted a job opening where Kelsey worked and enthused that you'd applied. It was shit work, but it would pay the bills and get you out of town. Maybe you two could be roommates.

Kelsey's fingers flew across the keyboard. "She was a high school friend. Very nice, but to be honest, I don't think she'd be a good fit. I'm not sure she's motivated enough for the demands of this position."

You round on Kelsey and in a fit of rage that surprises you, you shove her in the chest as hard as you can. She hits the wall hard. Rage shoves out fear and reason, and you want to hit her again. But Paige appears and grabs your arms. You breathe, close your eyes, unable to meet Kelsey's eyes.

"How could you?" The words catch in your throat.

"I don't know what the fuck that was, but it's not real," she splutters.

"What's going on?" Paige asks.

You open your eyes again. "I needed that job. I needed to get out of here. Out of my fucking parents' house. This shitty town. You knew. You *knew* how badly I needed that job. You knew this place was fucking killing me." You're screaming, though you hadn't meant to, and the words "fucking killing me" echo back to you through the empty bar as if mocking you.

"Jess is dead, and apparently we, or at least I, have a damn stalker, and you're making this about *you* right now? How about we escape this shitty karaoke bar and tell someone our friend is dead before we process our feelings, huh?" She turns her back on you.

Your hands clench into fists. You want to scream. You want to fight. You don't even know what you want her to do. Apologize? Fight back? Cry? Whatever it is you want right now, you're too angry to get any intelligible words out.

Kelsey glances over her shoulder at you. Her frizzy, orange hair is plastered to the sweat on her forehead, and she stares you dead in the eyes. "Let's split up and get this done faster."

"Fine by me." You don't wait for an answer as you climb up to the next floor, careful to step around Jess. Being alone in this place is terrifying, but you'll go completely mad if you look at

Kelsey's face for one more second.

Each room is the same. Empty, mildewed, and silent. You shut the last door in the stretch of hallway behind you and sit in the dark room. Too numb to cry in grief or rage like you think you should. A soft thump outside the door pulls you from your melancholy. You step out into the hall. You hear muffled shouting and then the sound of glass shattering. All thoughts leave your brain, and you run out of the room.

The bar has fallen silent. Your heart is pounding, and your mouth is dry as you creep down the hall, listening for every groan of settling wood and creaks of floorboards. When you reach the stairs, there are huge chunks of glass scattered on the steps, but you can't find the source. You race down the stairs into the main bar and look up.

On the top floor, instead of a brick wall, there is a panel of glass so people can look down on the stage below. In the center of the glass is a jagged, bloodied hole. You follow the path from the hole down to the ground floor and the stage just twenty feet in front of you.

You step carefully towards an unmoving, denim-clad shape laying almost exactly center stage. Your brain refuses to process what you're seeing. Blood and flesh and limbs jumbled and entwined in a way that looks like a curlycue ribbon on top of a fancy Christmas present. Orange hair lays in clumps around the macabre lump like confetti.

Footsteps echo down the stairs. You hear a gasp from your right. You turn to see Paige, her face pale and sweat slicked on her forehead. You stare at one another for a long moment. The questions "did she do this?" and "does she think I did this?" scream simultaneously through your head.

The screen behind the stage flicks to life, and this time, you feel something. A pull. Like a thin, warm blanket of static wrapped itself around your body and pulls you forward. It's you again. But a younger version. Driving your mom's beat-up sedan and thinking you were going to run away from home. You're too young yet to be driving legally, and you have a horrible feeling that you know what's about to happen. Something you shoved way down deep in your brain and only thought about when it jumped out at you in the middle of the night.

There's a flash in the road, and the car hits a bump that looks like a hiccup on screen. Such a small thing. But then you see young Kelsey crying. The only time you ever saw her do that. She'd come to you that night because you were the ear to listen and the shoulder to cry on, to tell you some monster had run over her cat and didn't even stop. You hate her a little bit that night. Crying about her cat while you wanted nothing more than to blast music through your headphones and cry alone in the dark because that thump under the tires had scared you so bad you turned around and went home.

You didn't know for sure that it was you who was the monster. But you never asked any questions that would confirm it, and you never told her. When the thought crosses your mind as an adult, you tell yourself it was fine. Even if you had hit Mr. Snowpants, as an even younger Kelsey had named him, you were a kid. You couldn't have been expected to do the right thing. But, Kelsey had never let her parents get another cat. The poor kid had been so fucking heartbroken.

Paige stares at you, her face twisted in shocked disgust. Even without words, without the memories you had, she'd put the pieces of what happened together. It had been hard to miss fourteen-year-old Kelsey's broken heart.

Had Kelsey seen what you just saw right before she died? Had she been pushed or had she fallen or jumped right after witnessing that act of betrayal? Had she had time to wonder what right you had to be angry with her for costing you a job after what you'd done?

You turn back to the pitiful wreck at your feet.

"Kelsey." Her name comes out like a command. As if by naming her, you could pull her body back into one piece.

As if you could pull your splintering life back into one piece.

I've been here for so long, waiting for someone to see me.
And still, you do not.

I hope I wasn't wrong about you.

5. SWEET DREAMS (ARE MADE OF THIS)

Paige sits across from you, silent. An air of distrust is palpable. You can't pretend Kelsey's death was misadventure or suicide. Not with you both having seen that video.

You want to ask Paige if she did it. But you can't make yourself say those words. Besides, you were the star or the villain of the piece in every video she'd seen. What right did you have to even think it might be her?

Paige glances up at you and back down to her hands, and you think she's wondering if you did it. It was impossible, you were nowhere near Kelsey when she fell, but you don't blame her. You'd fought, and now she's dead.

"There must be someone in here with us. If we just stay alert and together until morning—"

You laugh bitterly. "Look around. I don't know what the fuck is going on, but no one is coming tomorrow." You wave at the tray of nachos on the table in front of you. It's gone from moldy to a smear of black and green liquid in the time you'd sat at the table. Even the cardboard tray is disintegrating.

You see something move out of the corner of your eye. You turn to see a black shape roil and shift in front of the big television screen hanging over Kelsey's body. You squint, and it stops.

"Tell you what. I'm gonna take a piss. Coming?" Paige's voice is high and has too many jagged edges.

You can't let her go alone, so you follow.

If the bar is gross, the bathrooms are revolting. Thick, slick sheets of mold cover the walls and floor. The cracked, black mold encrusted sink hangs from the walls by the piping. Paige disappears into the least offensive stall.

She comes out. "Forgive me for not flushing." She laughs too loud.

The panic on her face brings a surge of love and protectiveness of your oldest friend rushing through the shocked numbness, and you grab her hand. The two of you have almost twenty years of crying, fighting, getting into and out of trouble together. It was shitty of you to even consider that she did this or even to think she suspects you. You trust her. She trusts you. You've had each other's back since forever. "It's going to be okay."

She gives you a wan, crooked smile. "I think it's already well past ever being okay again."

You open your mouth to respond when the moldy tile buckles under your feet. You shout and throw yourself backward, pulling Paige with you. But it's too late. The floor caves in beneath her.

Her hand is still clasped in yours. The jolt of her fall shoots up your arm, and there's a horrible pain in your shoulder, but you don't let go.

In vain, you try to find purchase with your toes on the mold-slicked floor, but Paige's weight drags you forward until you're half hanging over the lip of the hole.

You try to pull Paige up but can't, so you keep your grip tight and think. Below is a long drop into another karaoke room. It's dark in the way only a subterranean room can be and covered with the rotting remains of Halloween decorations and curling, mildewed posters for goth and metal bands. It's too far down, the ground too littered with broken furniture to drop her and hope for nothing more than a sprained ankle. But your shoulder is beginning to burn with agony, and there might not be a choice soon.

A bright light in the darkness catches your eye. With a hiss, the huge screen below her dangling feet comes to life. Paige's grip tightens.

At first, you think the video is nothing. High school Paige driving up to your house in her shitty, rust bucket of a car. But her eyes are furtive. Glancing at the windows of the house. Looking over her shoulder. She opens your mailbox. Sighs with what looks like relief. Gets in her car and drives away.

The scene repeats several times. Paige in different outfits each time. Different mail in the box, but she doesn't do anything.

Until the sixth time through, when she slides a large envelope out of the box. She opens her backpack and slips it inside. The scene skips to her sitting in her bedroom, perched on the edge of the bed like a nervous owl. She takes out the envelope and opens it. The stamp of the college letterhead at the top is unmistakable. As is the first sentence:

"Congratulations! We are pleased to invite you to join our fall class of entering freshmen... "

Rage rips you open and turns you completely inside out. Paige screams. You look at your now open hand in confusion. There's a crash and then silence. Distantly, you're aware of wet, burbling, strained breathing.

"Paige?" you whisper.

You race around the empty karaoke bar, trying to find the stairs that will lead you to where Paige fell. When at last you find them, the room is empty except for a few bloodstains and a huge, glowing screen.

It's your face on the screen, larger than life. It's impossibly shot from Paige's perspective. Her hand, white-knuckled and clenched around yours. The shot zooms into your face, at first determined and then twisted with rage.

The video repeats. Only this time, you see nothing but your hand clutching Paige's. And then it makes you watch as your fingers release, jerking out of Paige's desperate, frantic grasp. Over and over, the video plays, from all possible angles.

You step forward and press your forehead against the crackling screen. It's warm. That blanket of static envelopes you again, pulling you close. Holding you tight.

Now you know. Now you can't look away. You are the betrayed and the betrayer.

And you are just like me.

I've waited so long for you. We'll sing together. No secrets buried beneath the music; no betrayals hidden behind a smiling performance. Our voices are so perfectly matched.

I pull you deeper, deeper into yourself and into me you.

And finally, you see me.

ACKNOWLEDGEMENTS

A whole lot of people went into making this book, including all those who kept me relatively sane trying to write it during an absolute hellscape of a year. First, thanks to all the folks at TKO, especially Sebastian who both brought this project to me in the first place and was a most excellent editor.

A very special thanks to all my writer friends from the pub. Y'all are absolutely incredible humans and forever my writer family. Thank you so much for your support, listening to me vent, and celebrating with me. Special thanks to Ana Curtis for being a first reader on a story I was particularly flummoxed by and Caitlin Starling for helping me make some useful connections.

Thanks to Max Booth III who put out a call for an anthology and published one of my stories in it which through a series of events quite literally led to the existence of this book. Jordan Shiveley, spooky toothsome creator of dread extraordinaire, who helped me with titles and who once asked me if I was ever going to put out a collection and apparently the void listened.

Thank you to my parents who always kept me well stocked with horror books even if they sometimes (often) wondered why I was, and am, like this. To Libby, always my best friend and ready to listen or to distract as needed, thank you. Mama Rostholder, who has probably hand sold more of my books than I have, thanks as always for your support. Anya, the best dog in the world, who demanded I leave the house once in a while and occasionally flopped on top of my computer, I'd have been a more miserable person without you.

Lastly, thanks as always to Alison who was my unending source of love and support and provided reminders that sometimes I needed to eat some food and drink water. I could not have written this book without you.

– Leigh Harlen